Cheyenne Cowboy

Gat Hammer is a young cowboy who has decided to use his savings to buy himself a ranch as the cattle drive arrives in Dodge City. Having earned a big bonus, he deposits his wages in the town bank for safe-keeping. As the rest of his fellow wranglers paint Dodge red, Hammer rents a room in the Deluxe hotel, totally unaware of the fact that outlaw Emmett Holt and his gang are in town to rob the bank.

Wealthy lawyer Mason Dwire has planned and hired the Holt gang to make them all rich. It seems that nothing can stop the merciless bank robbers until young Hammer realizes that his savings have also been stolen. The Cheyenne cowboy gets riled and when his trail boss pal is gunned down in the shadows, he rides into action with guns blazing.

Cheyenne Cowboy

Max Gunn

A Black Horse Western

ROBERT HALE

© Max Gunn 2017
First published in Great Britain 2017

ISBN 978-0-7198-2126-4

The Crowood Press
The Stable Block
Crowood Lane
Ramsbury
Marlborough
Wiltshire SN8 2HR

www.bhwesterns.com

Robert Hale is an imprint
of The Crowood Press

Typeset by
Derek Doyle & Associates, Shaw Heath
Printed and bound in Great Britain by
CPI Group (UK) Ltd, Croydon, CR0 4YY

Dedicated to my father Denis
Vaya con Dios

PROLOGUE

A fiery glow spilled from the massive locomotive's smoke stack and lit up the night sky. It was an eerie sight as the massive locomotive forged on along the train tracks toward the railhead at Dodge City. Crimson sparks, like angry fireflies, pumped up into the darkness as clouds of black smoke billowed from its stack. The driver continued to look out from the train cab as his engineer shovelled coal and tossed lengths of wood into the open-jawed monster to feed its insatiable appetite.

A haunting sound hung over the vast land as the long caravan snaked on toward its destination. The mighty train relentlessly continued on for the distant Dodge City to load its empty cars with the steers that filled the famed railhead's stock pens.

Behind the powerful engine a string of empty

cattle cars screeched in the darkness as their wheels spat sparks and argued with the iron rails they were travelling along. Yet the last car was far from empty like all of the rest. This one had been commandeered by six ruthless individuals and their mounts who patiently waited for the hard-working locomotive to take them to their ultimate destination.

Red-hot sparks floated from the smoke stack into the crisp evening air whilst its brilliantly painted cowcatcher beneath the beam of its headlight ensured nothing would derail its charging bulk as it forged on toward the dimly lit watering station twenty miles east of the famed Dodge City.

Watering stations were essential for the locomotives in the searing heat of the desert plains. Their high towers filled with water pumped up from deep wells drew the precious liquid up so that it could be then fed into the bellies of the thirsty trains that travelled its tracks.

The station was similar to almost all its contemporaries and boasted a high tower topped by a huge water tower next to a windmill. Down at its base a small wooden structure housed the stationmaster and his telegraph key. Beside the tracks, countless poles stretched in both directions enabling men to communicate with one another regardless of the distance between them.

The car at the tail of the train was bathed in darkness and the familiar scent of nervous animals. The six horses and their hard-bitten riders were being carried in seclusion toward the prosperous settlement for a reason which only their leader knew.

Outlaw Emmett Holt was one of a rare breed of deadly men who plied their unforgiving trade in the ever-expanding West. For although his name was widely known throughout the states and territories, his actual likeness had never been either drawn or photographed.

Apart from those who hired or worked with him, nobody recognized his face when it bore down upon them. By then it was usually too late.

Holt liked it that way.

The five men who were travelling to Dodge City with Holt had no idea what they had been hired to do and yet they did not doubt that it would be profitable. Each of the men had total faith in Emmett Holt and knew that he would never accept any job if it were beyond their capabilities.

Holt had the ability to instil both loyalty and fear into those who rode with him. Few who had ever questioned his judgement ever lived long enough to boast about it and they all knew that simple fact. If you rode with Holt, you did what he said or suffered the consequences.

The sound of the locomotive cutting its way through the eerie landscape grew louder as it entered the canyon and reduced the distance between itself and the starlit water tower.

Only the howling of coyotes presented any rivalry to the clattering iron horse but even they could not compete with its train whistle.

The night air resounded sharply as the driver pulled on its cord several times to signal to the stationmaster of their imminent arrival. The driver and engineer leaned out from either side of the cab at the lantern light they were approaching. Moths were being plucked out of the air by bats as they encircled the glowing lights.

Brakes screeched as the locomotive slowed.

The haunting sound of the howling whistle alerted more than the ears of the stationmaster though. It also told Holt that they were nearing the place where he intended to disembark.

'Here we are, boys,' Holt said before scrambling to his feet and brushing the hay from his pants. 'By my figuring we're right on time.'

There were no disagreements.

The five other men rose from where they had been sitting on the floor of the car and moved to their mounts. Holt strode away from his men to the tall door and carefully slid it sideways. The lethal outlaw peered out of the sixteen-inch gap and grinned widely.

'Get the horses ready,' he grunted as his eyes focused on the fast-approaching station. 'When the train stops, we'll get these nags off this bone rattler.'

The station lights seemed brighter in the darkness of the canyon. Holt observed the engineer drop down from the cab, cross the tracks and start to climb the ladder up to where he could swing the water shoot over the engine. The train came to a shuddering halt, which vibrated along the numerous empty cars to where Holt and his men waited and watched.

'This is where we get off, boys,' Emmett Holt drawled without looking away from the water tower and the small wooden structure below it.

Bart Gibbs walked gingerly across the carriage floor until he was at Holt's shoulder. He squinted through the small gap and nodded in agreement.

'Where the hell are we, Emmett?' he wondered.

'Twenty miles east of Dodge, Bart,' Holt simply answered.

'How come we ain't travelling into town?' Gibbs scratched his chin.

Holt glanced at his underling. 'Because if we did that we'd be seen arriving by at least fifty hombres in the stockyard. I intend us riding in there just after sunrise. There ain't a whole lotta folks awake at that

11

time of day, boy. Savvy?'

Gibbs gave a fearful nod. 'I savvy.'

Holt turned, gripped the door and slid it wide open. 'C'mon, boys. Get the horses down out of here while them critters are quenching this train's thirst.'

The cool night air washed over the six men as they carefully led their mounts to the edge of the open cattle car and encouraged them to jump down.

Holt jumped to the ground and watched as his underlings continued to persuade their horses down from the car. Within less than a minute all six of their horses were on the ground beside the car.

'Check them cinch straps,' Holt growled as he rested his wrists on his gun grips and stared along the length of the caravan of stock cars.

The order had barely left his lips when the well-seasoned leader of the notorious gang moved away from the horses. He squinted hard at the train crew as they worked. Holt then glanced upward at the glistening telegraph wires that stretched from one pole to another as they went from the small building set beside the water tower in both directions.

'What you looking at, Emmett?' Gibbs piped up as he dropped his saddle fender and patted his horse's neck.

'Them wires,' Holt replied. He pulled a cigar from his pocket, bit off its tip and spat it at the dark sand.

Nothing ever escaped his knowing eyes as they observed everything that most men would not even notice. 'I'll have to do something about them.'

He struck a match across his belt buckle and cupped its flame to the end of the long black weed. As smoke billowed from his mouth, Gibbs moved to his side.

'What you gonna do, Emmett?' he asked.

The lethal leader of the small troop grunted as he silently tossed the match at the sand. Without uttering a word he pointed at the small building and then back at the wires that led to and from it.

Gibbs rubbed his whiskers. 'What about the telegraph wires? I don't savvy.'

Holt watched as the train whistle hooted and the powerful engine's wheels rotated on the steel tracks. Slowly the large iron horse began to move away from the water tower. Within seconds it had gathered speed and was disappearing into the black night.

'Folks talk on them wires, Bart,' Holt explained. 'Words travel faster than the fastest horse can gallop. We don't want anyone back in Dodge to go telling the rest of the territory what we just done, now do we?'

'I reckon not.' Gibbs shrugged. 'But we ain't done nothing yet.'

Emmett Holt rolled his eyes and inhaled on his

cigar deeply. He glanced at Gibbs. 'Don't go fretting, Bart. I'll do the thinking for all of us.'

Holt pulled the cigar from his lips and exhaled a line of smoke at the sand. He pushed his wide-brimmed Stetson back on to the crown of his head and glanced at the rest of his men.

'Before we head on down to Dodge I've got a job to do,' he drawled venomously.

They each looked at Holt as the hardened outlaw checked both his six-shooters in turn. None of them dared to ask what he intended to do because they already knew. Holt was staring at the small wooden structure with an evil grin etched into his features. He resembled a ravenous wolf eying its next prey.

'This shouldn't take too long,' Holt growled as he started toward the station building. The sound of his spurs chillingly echoed off the small building with the telegraph wires leading to and from its starlit features.

The outlaws held tightly on to the long leathers of their horses and watched as the deadly Holt advanced to the small structure and stepped up on to its boardwalk. The sound of creaking filled the barren surroundings as the outlaw leader moved to the small window. Lantern light from within the building washed over the lethal killer as his right hand dropped down to his holster and drew the long-barrelled weapon out. His thumb pulled back on its hammer until it clicked into position. Holt glanced at his small audience and grinned again.

'This'll be easy,' he sneered.

None of his gang uttered a word. They did not dare to for they each knew that Holt would not hesitate to turn his guns on them if they doubted his word. Holt smiled coldly through a cloud of smoke as his teeth gripped the long cigar.

Jim Dante, Slim Jones, Bud Collins, Bart Gibbs and Wes Harper watched as Holt turned the doorknob and hastily entered the station. He held his primed Colt at hip level and aimed its nickel-plated barrel at the tiny seated figure.

'Don't go moving, old timer,' Holt snarled.

The small man sat beside a desk with his hand poised above a telegraph key turned his swivel chair and looked up into the unshaven face of the outlaw.

'What do you want?' he gulped in shock before noticing the gun aimed straight at him. His lower lip began to shake as he vainly attempted to speak again.

Holt aimed his six-shooter at the head of the seated man and then squeezed his trigger. The small interior of the structure shook as a white flash spewed from the .45 and tore through his target's skull.

A plume of sickening gore exploded from the

hideous wound and plastered the wall in molten brain. Holt watched as it slowly slid down the wall behind the stricken man.

Holt blew the smoke from his gun barrel and grinned.

What was left of the stationmaster's head toppled off the chair with the rest of his body and landed at his executor's feet. Without a hint of emotion the deadly gunman holstered his smoking weapon and focused on the wall behind the telegraph key. Lumps of gore were slowly rolling down to the floor.

'That's not much of a brain, old timer,' he grinned before turning and walking back out into the cool night air. His eyes glanced at the faces of his followers as he holstered his still smoking gun.

He accepted his long leathers from Jones and swiftly stepped into his stirrup. Holt mounted the horse and gathered in his reins as his fellow killers followed his lead and also mounted.

'That was short and sweet, Emmett,' Gibbs said as he sat astride his muscular horse. 'Now what?'

Holt pointed at the telegraph wires. 'Shoot them down, boys. Shoot the whole bunch of them down.'

The five other mounted men drew their six-guns and aimed them skyward. The sound was deafening as the riders unleashed their guns' fury at the wires leading out of the small structure.

Within a matter of only seconds the telegraph wires had been severed and fell on to the sand. They dangled in the frosty starlight and swayed upon the ground. A satisfied smirk crossed Holt's face.

'Good. Now we can ride on to Dodge and get on with the job we've bin hired to do,' Holt said as Gibbs returned his cigar. 'With the wires cut there ain't no way that they'll be able to inform any of the surrounding towns about us. Nobody can talk to anybody now.'

'That means Dodge City is isolated,' Bud Collins grinned.

'Damn right.' Holt nodded as he patted the neck of his horse. 'And by the time they fix them wires we'll be long gone.'

The five riders drew level with their leader and looked at the merciless horseman. None of them spoke as Holt stood in his stirrups and pointed down the rail tracks.

'Let's ride, boys,' Holt spat before whipping the shoulders of his mount. The startled animal jolted into action. Within seconds the rest of his gang were in hot pursuit. 'Now we can do what we've bin paid to do.'

The canyon walls echoed with the thundering sound of the horses' hoofs as all six of their mounts raced beside the tracks. Emmett Holt had eliminated

17

the possibility of Dodge City communicating with the outside world. Now the sprawling settlement was at the mercy of the six riders but like so many of their breed, they never showed anyone or anything mercy.

ONE

His name was Gat Hammer but most knew him simply as the Cheyenne cowboy. Hammer had earned the respect of most of his fellow wranglers over the years for his prowess and skill in handling all four-legged animals. As his nickname implied Hammer hailed from Cheyenne and since childhood had worked hard at being the best he could be.

The trail drive he had worked as scout and lead wrangler for the previous three months had just filled the stock pens at the Dodge City railhead with five thousand white-faced steers. It had grown dark in the sprawling town before the wranglers and crew had been paid off but the glowing lantern lights made Dodge seem even more inviting.

Hammer had been paid his wages plus a handsome bonus for expertly doing his job better than anyone else. Yet the allure of Dodge held no interest for the cowboy for this was the tenth time he had visited the famed town.

For most cowboys as young as the twenty-two-year-old this was a time to get liquored up and finally let your hair down, but not for Hammer. The youngster, who most considered at least a decade older than he actually was, had decided upon a far more sober way to spend his first night of relative freedom.

The Cheyenne cowboy did not want to chase the many working females who flocked to and filled the bars closest to the rail tracks, nor did he want to drink himself senseless either. He had other plans. Caked in trail dust, both horse and master headed slowly away from the activity of the stock pens and he guided his mount toward the heart of Dodge City. The haunting sound of a locomotive whistle filled the evening air behind him as Hammer continued on into the heart of the large town.

He crossed the wide main street and pulled his highly trained cutting horse to a halt outside the best of the settlement's hotels.

Hammer glanced up at the board above the porch. The Deluxe Hotel was every bit as classy as its name implied. This would be the first time that the cowboy had ever chosen to stay within its fancy walls.

He could hear the rest of the trail hands whooping

as they thundered past him on their way to the many saloons. He shook his head and sighed. He had done that too many times himself but not tonight.

For Hammer, the thought of a hot bath and a clean bed far outweighed anything else the prosperous Dodge City had to offer. He raised himself up and off his high-shouldered mount and rested beside the handsome animal.

'Easy, Flame,' he said to the white-faced chestnut stallion as he stepped toward the long hitching rail. He looped his long leathers over the pole and then secured them with a slip knot. 'I'll make sure you get rubbed down and well fed before I sink my aching bones into that tub.'

The stallion snorted as its master pulled his saddlebags free and placed them over his wide shoulder. He patted the horse and climbed the three steps up to the freshly painted front door of the hotel. Hammer reached down to the brass doorknob and entered.

The bright lamplight in the hotel lobby made Hammer squint as he walked across to the highly decorative desk. He knew that he looked out of place in such elegant surroundings but he had bonus money in his shirt pocket and that made him the equal of the hotel's more refined guests.

'Can I help you?' a rather pompous desk clerk

21

asked him as he rested his gloved hands on the desk. 'The saloons are down the street. This is the Deluxe. I think it might not be in your price range, young man.'

The cowboy smiled. Hammer was not easily riled.

'I want a room and a tub full of hot soapy water,' he drawled down at the far shorter man on the other side of the desk. 'I also want a steak dinner and someone to take my horse down to the livery for me.'

The clerk cleared his throat and leaned across his open register. 'You don't seem to understand. This is the Deluxe Hotel. We are very expensive.'

Hammer leaned across the desk counter as well. The brim of his Stetson touched the clerk's highly polished head. 'You're the one who seems confused, partner. I've got the money and I want all the things I just told you about. Savvy?'

The clerk was about to speak again when his eyes widened at the sight of the wad of bills in the cowboy's hand as Hammer started to peel them off and place them on top of the ledger.

'A room, you said?' The clerk repeated the Cheyenne cowboy's words. 'And a tub of soapy water? Certainly.'

'Hot soapy water, friend.' Hammer smiled. 'How much will that be?'

The drooling clerk scooped up the bank notes

eagerly and pocketed them. He turned the register around, dipped a pen in the ink well and handed it to Hammer.

'This will cover it,' he gushed.

The Cheyenne cowboy grinned. 'I'm sure it will.'

'I'll get the boy to take your horse to the stable and have the chef prepare your steak before you reach your room.' The older man glanced down at the register. 'I hope you'll enjoy your stay, Mr Hammer.'

The cowboy placed the pen down and accepted the key. 'I'm sure I will.'

The clerk watched as the cowboy approached the flight of stairs. With every step he left trail dust. The balding man cleared his throat just loud enough to draw Hammer's attention to him as he placed a boot upon the bottom step of the staircase.

'May I make a suggestion, Mr Hammer?' the squeaky voice asked as the cowboy looked in his direction.

'You sure can, friend.' Hammer smiled. 'I'm listening.'

'We have an excellent cleaning service,' the clerk stammered nervously. 'We could clean your clothes while you are having your soak in the tub. They'll be fresh and dry by the morning.'

Hammer nodded. 'That's a good idea. The hombre who brings up the hot water for the tub can collect my duds.'

The clerk watched as Hammer continued on up to the second floor. With each step the sound of his spurs rang out around the lobby. When the cowboy was no longer in sight he pulled out the bills and smiled at them.

'What a pleasant young man,' he drooled again as he stared at the bank notes in his hands. 'Dusty, but nice.'

TWO

Dodge City was filled with the sound of awakening roosters as they greeted the rising sun. Gat Hammer yawned and rubbed the sleep from his eyes and then stared around the well-appointed hotel room. He inhaled deeply and then threw the bedsheets off his bruised body. The cowboy rose up and dropped both his legs on to the carpeted floor as he slowly gathered his wits.

Sunlight defied the window drapes and bathed the room in a golden glow. The Cheyenne cowboy reached to the bedpost and pulled his saddle-bag toward him. He unbuckled its satchels and extracted a clean pair of pants and a shirt, which he quickly slipped on.

Tucking his shirt into his buttoned pants he then snaked his belt through its loops and secured the buckle. Hammer had no sooner done this than he heard a gentle rap on the door.

His eyes flashed to the freshly painted door.

'Who is it?' he called out across the room.

'The bellhop, sir,' came the reply. 'I've brung your clean clothes. You want me to leave them out here in the hall?'

Hammer pulled the door toward him and stared at the short youngster holding the freshly pressed clothing in his hands. As the cowboy reached down and took the clothes, he noticed that the boy was no more than twelve and covered in freckles.

'Thanks, son,' Hammer drawled before moving to the dresser where he had piled his personal items the night before. He slid a quarter into the palm of his hand and then laid the clothes down on the highly polished surface. Hammer turned and walked across the carpeted floor and then gave the boy the coin. 'There you go.'

'A quarter.' The youngster smiled at the coin. 'Gee, thanks. Anything else you want? You want a woman? I know them all.'

Hammer chuckled. 'I'm sure you do but I'm not looking for any female company at the moment.'

The boy raised his eyebrows. 'Anything else?'

'Come to think about it, there is.' The cowboy rubbed his stomach. 'Is there any chance of getting some grub, son? I know it's early but my innards are grumbling.'

The boy nodded. 'The cook has just started rustling up vittles, mister. Do you want to eat in the dining room or do you want me to bring up a tray of grub here?'

Hammer still did not feel as though he should be staying in such a classy hotel and shrugged. He looked down at his bare feet and then at the young worker.

'Could you bring me eggs and bacon and a pot of coffee, son?' he asked the smiling boy. 'I don't feel that cowboys fit these surroundings. I'd rather eat up here.'

'No problem.' The boy winked. 'I'll bring you everything. Bacon, eggs, biscuits and a pile of pancakes should fill your belly just fine, mister.'

Hammer smiled broadly. 'Hell. That sounds real good.'

The boy turned and then looked over his shoulder. 'My name's Billy. Billy Vine.'

'My name's . . .' Hammer did not manage to finish his statement. The boy had run down the corridor and disappeared before the cowboy had time to give him his name. He closed the door and moved to his clean socks. 'Friendly little critter.'

THREE

The rising sun hung over the massive range as the six horsemen guided their mounts to a halt on a dusty ridge. Emmett Holt leaned on his saddle horn and stared down at the sprawling city and then at his men. He raised a hand and pointed at the sight that greeted them and then smiled.

'Look at them stock pens, boys,' he drawled as he located another fat cigar and bit off its tip. 'Have you ever seen so much beef?'

Gibbs lowered his canteen from his mouth. Droplets of water ran from the corners of his lips as he screwed its stopper.

'Is that what we gotta do, Emmett?' he asked. 'Have we gotta steal them steers?'

Holt glanced at Gibbs. 'Nope, that ain't why we're here, Bart. Besides, what the hell would we do with a couple of thousand steers?'

Gibbs nodded. 'They would be kinda hard to hide.'

Holt scratched a match across the top of his saddle horn and then cupped the flame to his cigar. He inhaled the smoke deeply and tossed the match at the ground. The gleaming rail tracks glistened like a string of diamonds as they led down to Dodge. His smile grew wider as he finally allowed the smoke to escape his lips. His eyes narrowed as they watched the massive locomotive wind its way into the outskirts of the famed settlement and finally entered the enormous stockyards. Black smoke puffed up into the cloudless blue sky from the locomotive's black stack. From their vantage point they could see the entire city.

'It's still mighty early, boys,' Holt told them as he gathered the loose ends of his long leathers in his gloved left hand. 'Nobody will notice us when we enter Dodge. That's exactly the way I want it. We keep our heads low until I find out exactly what the job is. No fights. We don't wanna draw unwanted eyes.'

Jim Dante scratched his head before lowering his Stetson back down on to his grey hair. He leaned forward and looked along the line of horsemen at Holt.

'I figured that you knew what it was we were hired to do, Emmett,' he croaked. 'Are you telling us that you ain't got any notion what we're meant to do?'

Holt glanced along the line of riders at Dante. 'Shut the hell up or I'll part your head with a bullet, Jim. Savvy?'

Dante went silent and slumped back on to his saddle.

Holt gripped his cigar between his teeth and whipped the shoulders of his mount.

'C'mon,' the deadly outlaw shouted over his wide shoulder as he raced down the ridge beside the steel rail tracks. 'We got us work down yonder.'

A mere heartbeat later, the five other outlaws raced after Holt. All they knew for certain was that somewhere in Dodge City there was a job to do and they were going to do it.

FOUR

Billy returned to the hotel room less than ten minutes after he had hurriedly departed. In his hands he expertly balanced a large silver tray laden down with everything he had promised the cowboy. He gently kicked the room door and held his fragrant cargo between his hands. Hammer opened the door and ushered the bellhop into the room.

'You're mighty fast, Billy,' the Cheyenne cowboy grinned.

'Where'd you want this?' Billy asked as Hammer pulled on his high-sided boots and stomped on the floor until satisfied that they were comfortable. 'I asked you where you wanted me to put these vittles. They're real heavy.'

There was something about the kid that Hammer liked. Billy Vine had spirit and that sat well with the

31

cowboy. He raised an arm and pointed at the table near the window.

'Over there,' Hammer said. He trailed the lad as his aromatic breakfast was carefully placed down.

'Sure looks good,' Billy said staring hungrily at the food he had just delivered. 'The cook really knows how to rustle up breakfast.'

The cowboy nodded in agreement. 'He sure does. I've never seen food look so neat before. Smells real good too.'

Billy glanced out of the window at the sun-baked street and then over at the buildings opposite. The black smoke from the trail curled up in the distance. 'They'll have them steers loaded in no time, I bet.'

'I reckon so.' Hammer smiled.

'We get trail herds in here every week nowadays,' Billy informed him. 'Them folks back east can't seem to get enough of the cattle you and your friends bring here.'

Hammer remembered that he had not had time to tell Billy his own name earlier. He cleared his throat.

'I was gonna tell you my name when you high-tailed it, Billy,' Hammer said as he sat down before his piping hot breakfast.

Billy glanced back out of the window at the quiet street. The rising sun was starting to awaken the townsfolk and draw them from their individual hiding places. The youngster looked back at the cowboy.

'There ain't no need. Everybody knows who you are,' Billy grinned. 'You're the Cheyenne cowboy folks are talking about.'

The cowboy raised an eyebrow and studied his young friend as Billy placed his hands on the backrest of his padded chair and watched as Hammer looked in awe at the meal before him.

'I am?' Hammer replied.

'You are the Cheyenne cowboy, ain't you?' Billy repeated before moving around the table and seating himself opposite.

Hammer nodded. 'That's what they call me but I didn't know that anyone, apart from my fellow cowpunchers, knew me around these parts. Who in tarnation has bin talking about me?'

'Everybody.' Billy reached across the table to the tray and lifted one of the slices of toast from the rack. He started to bite and chew it. 'Sure wish I was a cowboy like you, Cheyenne.'

The cowboy grinned. 'I was about as big as you when I went on my first trail drive. Must be about seven or eight years back, I guess.'

'Golly gee,' Billy gasped excitedly. 'Does that mean I could be a cowboy like you, Cheyenne?'

'Reckon so.' Hammer removed a folded napkin

from the tray and tucked it into the neck of his buttoned shirt. His mind frantically tried to work out how anyone could possibly know who he was. As far as he knew, he was just another drover at the end of a long trail drive. Hammer poured coffee into the white china cup.

'Do you reckon you could put a good word in for me, Cheyenne?' Billy asked as he finished the last of his toast and hopped back on to his feet. 'I sure would like to be a cowboy like you.'

'It's a hard life, Billy,' Hammer sighed. 'Brutal at times.'

'I don't care.' Billy grinned.

'You gotta be able to ride, Billy,' Hammer said as he cut the eggs apart so that their golden yoke filled the plate.

'I can ride.' Billy started for the room door as he rubbed the crumbs off his mouth. 'We got us a mule. I've bin riding that critter for years. Bareback.'

'Bareback?' The cowboy smiled as he ate. 'I'm impressed. I'll have a word with the trail boss. He might hire you but it ain't no picnic being a cowpuncher.'

Billy had crossed the room. He paused, looked back at his hero and grabbed hold of the doorknob. 'I'd sure be grateful if you could help me, Cheyenne. I'd hate to waste my whole life working in the Deluxe.'

Hammer could understand. As Billy left the room he smiled to himself. The kid reminded him of how he used to be. He sprinkled sugar into his cup and glanced at the window to the sun-drenched street below his room. The steam of the beverage filled his nostrils as he took a sip. It reminded him what real coffee was meant to taste like and bore no resemblance to the beverage he was used to, dished up from a chuck wagon. He was about to swallow when long morning shadows traced across the sand of the main thoroughfare.

He could tell it was horsemen. Quite a lot of horsemen.

The curious cowboy allowed the coffee to find its way down into his gullet and then rose back to his full height and stepped closer to the window. With the cup still in his hand he pressed his temple against the glass as six horsemen came into view.

A cold shiver traced down his spine.

He watched them carefully steer their lathered-up horses along the still quiet street toward the livery stable at the far end.

'Now who in tarnation are those hombres?' he asked himself before returning to his chair and resting himself down upon its padded seat. He placed the cup down upon its saucer and then lifted the cutlery and started to cut up the still sizzling bacon.

As he chewed and savoured the taste of well-cooked food, his mind raced. There was something about the six riders that did not sit well with Hammer.

He knew what the average cowboy looked like and those men were definitely not cut from their cloth. Hammer made short work of the meal as he dwelled upon the thought of the half-dozen horsemen and tried to work out why they made him so uneasy. Folding the last slice of bread he mopped up every last drop of the yoke.

Hammer washed the unexpectedly good meal down his throat with a mouthful of the black coffee. He became convinced that the six horsemen were either lawmen or they were hired gunmen. It seemed doubtful that they were star packers. He patted the sides of his mouth with the napkin and then pulled it free of his shirt collar.

Hammer stood, tossed the cloth on top of the plate and then strode across the room to where his six-shooter hung in its holster. He lifted the gunbelt free of the bedpost and strapped it around his hips.

The cowboy moved to his saddlebag and unbuckled one of its satchel flaps. He pulled out a bank book and his trail drive earnings. As was his ritual, he was going to deposit the cash in the bank and use the remainder of his handsome bonus money to live on.

That was his plan anyway.

He slid the bank book into his shirt pocket with the folded cash and smiled to himself.

'Reckon I'll go put a good word in for little Billy before the bank opens,' he muttered before picking up his still dusty hat and placing it over his hair. He rubbed his face, then glanced in the stand mirror and sighed at his reflection. 'Sure wish I could grow me some damn whiskers.'

The Cheyenne cowboy exited the room, locked its door and hastily made his way to the top of the staircase. He descended the steps and moved across the lobby toward the slumbering clerk propped on his chair behind the desk. The man was dozing on his chair as the cowboy slapped the palm of his hand on the wooden counter top.

The noise resonated around the hotel lobby.

The startled clerk awoke suddenly and stared at the tall Hammer who was looking down at him. A feeble smile etched the face of the slightly built man as he got to his feet and yawned.

'Can I help you, Mr Hammer?'

'I'd like to rent that room for another day, partner.' Hammer smiled as he placed another greenback on the register and pushed it toward the clerk. 'Unless you got any objections, that is?'

'Absolutely no objections, my dear sir.' The clerk

scooped up the five-dollar bill and clutched it to his chest. 'None at all.'

Hammer was about to turn when he recalled the words little Billy Vine had uttered up in his room. He rested a hand on the desk counter.

'Tell me something, friend,' the cowboy enquired. 'Are folks talking about me?'

The clerk shrugged. 'I don't know.'

'Folks are said to be talking about the Cheyenne cowboy,' Hammer added. 'Some hombres call me that.'

The clerk shook his head. 'I've not heard anything but I ain't bin out of the Deluxe since yesterday. If I do hear of anyone talking about you, I'll ask why.'

Hammer sighed heavily.

'Thanks, friend. I'm going to stretch my legs.' Hammer touched the brim of his hat, swung on his heels and walked with dogged determination out into the bright street.

He closed the hotel door behind him and then looked to his left and then to his right. Dodge City was eerily quiet for a town with so many cowboys within its boundaries. Hammer narrowed his eyes and stared down at the six horsemen outside the livery. Something was still gnawing at his craw. It was an uneasy feeling that Hammer could neither understand nor fully explain.

Hammer knew only too well that sometimes you could sense trouble a long time before it actually happens. That was the feeling he had as he watched the six dust-caked horsemen outside the tall livery stable. The overwhelming feeling of impending danger.

'Who the hell are those hombres?' he sighed as he rubbed his jaw thoughtfully. 'They sure look like trouble to me. Mighty big trouble.'

The cowboy shook his head and then diverted his eyes from the men who troubled him. He then remembered his promise to the young bellhop. Billy wanted to be a cowboy and Hammer was respected enough by his fellow cowpunchers to put a good word in for the youngster.

Gat Hammer had a fair idea where he would find most of his fellow drovers but was not quite so sure about the whereabouts of trail boss, Tom McGee. McGee was a man of many moods. He could drink most towns dry but sometimes satisfied his thirst with soda pop.

The Cheyenne cowboy wondered which McGee he was looking for. Was it the mad womanizing drunk or the calm professional? He rubbed the nape of his neck and then heard the familiar sound of his fellow cowboys' raised voices coming from a saloon two hundred yards from where he stood.

A liquor-fuelled fight seemed to be in full flow.

'Maybe the boys know where Tom is,' Hammer muttered as he aimed his boots toward the boisterous sound and hurried toward the saloon. The closer he got, the louder the noise became. The cowboy jumped down from the boardwalk and raced across the sand. He quickly mounted the steps to the next boardwalk. As he narrowed the distance between himself and the saloon he cast his attention at the large brick and stone bank opposite.

That would be his next destination after he found McGee, he thought. He would pay his trail drive earnings into the bank account he had opened three years earlier. Finally he would have enough money saved to buy himself a small spread and raise his own cattle.

The thought appealed to Hammer. Being a cowboy was a romantic profession but it was also a hard one. He had lost count how many of his fellow cowboys had been either crippled or killed since his first cattle drive. It was a job that did not take prisoners.

One mistake was usually your last.

Hammer looked up at the rowdy saloon he was quickly approaching when the large window beside him shattered into a million fragments as a man hurtled through it. The startled cowboy swung on his heels and stared at the bleeding man on the ground. He pushed the swing doors apart and entered the saloon.

The smell of stale sweat and other bodily fluids greeted the cowboy. He rubbed his nose and squinted into the dimly lit room as men fought feverishly. He knew most of them.

'Hi, boys,' Hammer called out and made his way to the long bar counter.

The words had no sooner left his lips than a chair flew just past his head. Hammer ducked as the chair skidded along the bar counter and crashed through a pyramid of whiskey glasses. Shattering glass rang out like the tolling of bells. Hammer stepped toward the counter as the battle continued. He touched his hat brim at the nervous bartender.

'Howdy, barkeep.' He smiled. 'Have you seen the hombre in charge of these galoots?'

'You mean that old drunk cowboy with the handlebar moustache?' the shaking man answered as his unblinking eyes watched the fight that had already destroyed half the saloon's furniture and looked as though it was hell-bent on turning what was left into matchwood. 'That bastard bought his boys a whiskey each and then downed a whole bottle himself. These critters have bin fighting all night.'

'Any notion where I might find the drunk with the

handlebar moustache?' Hammer asked as he tossed a coin into the fearful bartender's hands. 'I'm looking for him.'

The bartender stared long and hard at the cowboy.

'Why'd a nice clean-cut hombre like you want to find him for?' he asked. 'You don't wanna go getting mixed up with their kind. They're cowboys.'

A scream drew both men's eyes to the corner. They watched as one of the saloon's patrons was lifted off the ground and tossed into an upright piano. White and black keys flew up into the air as the body crashed into it. A morbid tune rang out.

'Cowboys?' Hammer jested. 'Scum of the earth.'

'Damn right, son.' The bartender nodded at Hammer. 'Look at them. They're animals, boy. The same thing happens every time they bring a herd in. You don't wanna get mixed up with their kind.'

The Cheyenne cowboy nodded. 'You're right. I'd best go before I get hurt. You don't happen to know where the drunk with the handlebar moustache went, do you?'

'He left with Montana Mae,' the bartender replied. 'They were both liquored up and panting like hound dogs, if you get my drift.'

'Tom sure must have bin real liquored up to go with Montana,' Hammer grinned at the bartender. He touched his hat brim and was making his way back to the swing doors when two brawling men crashed into him. The Cheyenne cowboy staggered as one of the bruised and bloodied men held the other by his bandanna and then sent a fist into his teeth. The sound of breaking ivory filled the room as the man looked at Hammer and smiled.

'Howdy, Cheyenne.' His fellow drover grinned through blood and bruises before releasing his grip on his sleeping opponent. 'Ain't seen you for ages. Where've you bin?'

'Sleeping.' Hammer smiled and watched as his saddle pal raced back into the heart of the fight. He looked at the confused bartender and shrugged. 'We go to the same church and sing in the choir,' he lied.

After watching Hammer exit the debris-littered saloon the bartender rolled up his sleeves, picked up a three-foot-long length of lumber and gripped it in his hands. The bartender strode along through the debris behind the counter and emerged amid the continuing destruction.

'Will you boys quit busting up my saloon?' he yelled at the brawling men. There was no response to his plea. Men kept fighting and remnants of furniture kept flying in all directions.

The bartender lowered his head and started to snort like a raging bull. His hands tightened their

43

grip on the length of lumber.

'To hell with it,' he yelled as he ploughed into the bloodied cowboys.

FIVE

The morning sun bathed the six riders in its golden glow as the half-dozen men studied the towering edifice before them with calculating eyes. One by one the horsemen moved the noses of their mounts closer to the fragrant structure and looked into its hollow depths. Emmett Holt dismounted and handed his reins to Jim Dante before dusting his trail gear down with his gloved hands. The outlaw leader pointed up at Gibbs and then aimed his trigger finger at the water pump beside a long trough.

'Fill the canteens, Bart,' he muttered before hearing the solid steps of the liveryman walking out of the shadows behind his broad shoulders. 'I don't want us wasting time when it's time for us to leave this town.'

Gibbs looped his leg over the neck of his mount

45

and then dropped to the ground as he saw the black-smith striding out into the morning light. He turned to the rest of the horseman and gritted his teeth.

'You heard Emmett,' he snarled. 'Fill the canteens.'

'Who the hell are you?' Clem Barker the blacksmith asked as his eyes studied the six men who confronted him. 'I don't recall there being a circus due in Dodge.'

The remark would usually have been enough for Holt to draw his gun and start shooting but the hired gunman was too slick for that. He wanted his men to keep a low profile until they had fulfilled their work in Dodge City. No amount of insults would arouse his infamous anger. Somehow Holt forced a smile while turning to face Barker.

'I want these nags fed and watered, amigo,' he growled.

Barker walked his bulk around the six horses. With every step his large head nodded. These were no normal saddle horses, he thought. These were top grade animals and far too good for the bunch who seemed to own them. He paused beside Holt and rubbed his sweating chins.

'Where'd you get this horseflesh?' he asked the outlaw.

Holt stared from under the brim of his hat at the

man who glistened in the powerful rays of the sun. He had never seen so much muscle in one place before.

'Why'd you ask, *amigo?*'

One of Barker's busted eyebrows rose as he looked at the obviously dangerous leader of the bunch. 'I was just gonna tell you that I've never seen such fine horseflesh in years.'

Barker paused for a moment and then added to his statement. He swung his body around and pointed inside his stable.

'Mind you, one of the hotel boys brung a mighty fine flame-faced stallion in here last night,' he sighed. 'That horse is bigger than any of these animals but I reckon your horses could outrun the critter.'

Holt looked to where the stableman was indicating and without uttering a word he strode into the shadows and then halted. His eyes adjusted to the far darker interior of the livery as he searched the stalls for the distinctive flame-faced horse the liveryman had mentioned.

Then he saw it.

'Fine animal, ain't it?' Barker said as he moved to Holt's shoulder and tucked his thumbs into his broad black leather belt. 'The boy told me it belongs to a cowboy.'

Holt glanced at Barker. 'A cowboy, you say?'

Barker nodded. 'Yep. The kid reckoned it was the critter they call the Cheyenne cowboy. I ain't ever heard of him but the boy said he was famous. Have you heard of him?'

Emmett Holt sighed heavily. 'I've heard of him.'

The blacksmith took his eyes from the handsome mount and stared at the outlaw. He tilted his head slightly.

'You sound kinda regretful, mister,' he noted.

Holt drew breath through his gritted teeth. 'You might say that. I've run up against the Cheyenne cowboy before. That young bastard is damn good with his six-shooter considering he's just a cow-puncher.'

'Did you tussle with him?' Barker's curiosity was growing.

'Yep.' Holt turned on his heels, then pulled a cigar from his pocket and bit off its black tip. He spat at the dirt floor and placed the smoke between his lips.

'You sound like a critter that got himself bad memories of this Cheyenne fella,' Barker said as he watched the grim-faced outlaw signal for his men to lead their horses into the livery stable.

Emmett Holt pulled a golden eagle from his vest pocket and tossed the coin into the muscular hands. 'We got unfinished business, *amigo*.'

48

Barker bit the gleaming golden coin and then slipped it into his apron pocket. 'How long do you wanna have me look after these horses of yours?'

Holt struck a match and slowly sucked its flame into the fat cigar. He held it in his lungs thoughtfully and then started to walk back toward the sunlight. Smoke trailed over his shoulder as he reached the blinding rays of the street.

'How long do you want me to tend to these animals?' Barker repeated as the rest of the gang followed their leader. 'This twenty-dollar piece is enough to last the longest time. How long do you figure?'

Holt glanced over his shoulder. His ice-cold stare caught the large liveryman by surprise. For the first time in a long while, Barker was afraid.

'Just rub them nags down then water and feed them,' the ruthless outlaw said through a cloud of smoke. 'I'll let you know when we're leaving town when I know myself.'

Barker nodded fearfully.

Holt then raised his hand and added, 'Which hotel is the cowboy staying at?'

'The Deluxe,' the large man answered.

Holt nodded and then led his men out into the blinding light. Within seconds they were gone but it would take a lot longer for the blacksmith to forget

49

the fear that Holt's eyes had burned into him.

'Who the hell is this Cheyenne cowboy critter, Emmett?' Wes Harper asked the tall emotionless Holt as they strode along the sun-drenched street toward the heart of Dodge.

'He made a name for himself killing three of my boys last summer, Wes,' Holt snarled as his teeth tightened on the cigar. 'Got himself in all the papers.'

The men flanking the tall outlaw could hear the anger in Holt's voice as he recalled his previous encounter with the man known as the Cheyenne cowboy.

'What you figuring on doing, Emmett?' Gibbs asked as they all stepped up on the boardwalk outside a hardware store.

Holt glanced at Gibbs but did not reply.

SIX

With each passing second Dodge was becoming busier. Yet within the confines of the narrow passage-ways of the Rialto Boarding House it remained eerily dark. The Rialto was a place where few cared for lux-uries like windows for there was little any of the females within its walls had time to look at besides the money in their clients' hands.

Hammer found it hard to believe that it was early morning as he ascended the creaking stairs to the second floor. With every room door closed, it was darker than an outside privy on a moonless night. He paused at the end of the corridor and screwed up his eyes until they finally managed to focus.

He counted eight doors. Four to either side. By the sound of laughter, giggling and satisfied male grunts that emanated along the dark passage, the cowboy knew he was close to his trail boss.

Hammer started to walk slowly. With every step he tilted his head and listened for a clue as to McGee's location. After he had travelled to virtually the end of the narrow confines of the hastily constructed corridor he heard the familiar sound of a hacking cough.

The Cheyenne cowboy paused and strained to hear voices more clearly when suddenly the room door abruptly opened and the barrel of a Remington .44 was pushed up into his throat.

'Who the hell are you?' the growling voice asked as he heard the distinctive sound of the gun's hammer being cocked under his chin. 'Answer me before I blow your head off your shoulders. Are you some kinda pervert? The kind that gets their kicks from listening to folks enjoying themselves? Are you?'

It was the voice of McGee. A rather exhausted voice, but it definitely belonged to the trail boss. Hammer swallowed hard as he felt the cold steel push his head back under his Stetson.

'It's me, Tom,' he croaked and wished it was not quite so dark along the corridor. 'I got me a favour to ask you.'

The gun was lowered as quickly as it had been raised. Hammer could smell McGee's liquor-flavoured breath on his face as the trail boss moved closer.

'Gat?' McGee groaned. 'Is that you?'

Hammer nodded his head and carefully pushed the six-shooter aside. 'It sure is, Tom. Just little old me.'

'What you doing creeping up and down here for?' McGee asked as he made his way back into the dimly lit room and rested his naked backside on the bed.

'Can I pull the drapes, Tom?' Hammer asked. 'The room is real dark.'

The veteran cowpuncher glanced over his shoulder at the snoring female and winced. 'Leave the damn drapes the way they are, Gat. I don't feel strong enough to cast my eyes on Montana Mae right now.'

Even the half-light could not hide the truth from the cowboy's eyes. The female was not exactly easy to look at when she was covered in thick make-up and doused in perfume but after romping around on her well-exercised bed, and covered in sweat, her own as well as her client's, she was not easy to look at.

'Feeling better?' Hammer asked his boss as he glanced around the pitiful room and the few personal items belonging to Mae. 'Me and the boys noticed you've bin a tad tense the last couple of days.'

McGee glanced up at the cowboy.

'Whatever it is that you want, Gat,' he growled wearily, 'it better be good. Damn good. I'm tuckered

53

but I still got enough vinegar in me to kick your sorrowful ass.'

'I was wondering if you might be hiring new hands for the ride back home, Tom,' the cowboy said above the loud snores of the female.

McGee laughed and shook his head. 'Only you would choose to ask that question at a time like this, Gat. I've just strained every muscle I've got and you come asking dumb questions like that.'

'I had to ask you before you left Dodge, Tom,' Hammer explained. 'You see, I won't be going back with you this time, boss.'

The trail boss sat upright and looked at his top wrangler with a stunned expression carved into his face. 'What you mean, Gat? You're quitting?'

Hammer walked over to the window and pulled the thin drape across. Sunlight filled the room as the cowboy stared out at the back streets.

'I've got me enough saved now, Tom,' he told the older man. 'More than enough to buy me that little spread I've bin hankering over for the last few years.'

The room fell into silence for a few moments. The only sound was coming from the other engaged rooms along the passageway. The Cheyenne cowboy just stared out of the window and listened as his friend and mentor struck a match and the room filled with the aroma of cigar smoke.

'I'll miss you, Gat,' McGee finally said. 'You've bin like a son to me. You're the only one in the bunch that I've always bin able to trust.'

'Likewise, Tom.' The cowboy turned and walked through the smoke back to the open door. His left hand gripped its woodwork as he paused and looked down upon his boss. 'But it's time for me to try and start up my own spread. If I fail I'll come begging for my job back.'

McGee looked up through the grey smoke between them.

'You'll not fail, boy.' He grinned. 'When you set your mind to something, you never fail.'

The Cheyenne cowboy grinned back. 'I appreciate that.'

The older man covered his modesty with part of the bed sheet and tapped the ash from his cigar. He raised his eyebrows high and smiled at Hammer.

'Why'd you ask if I was hiring, Gat?' he asked.

'There's a young kid over in the hotel,' Hammer said. 'He wants to be a cowboy more than anything, Tom. I told him that I'd put a good word in. He's keen and I've got me a feeling that he'll be a real good cowboy given a chance.'

'Just like you were,' McGee remembered. 'What's this kid's name, Gat?'

'Billy Vine.' Hammer touched the brim of his hat

and stepped out of the room. As he gripped the doorknob he looked at the trail boss again. 'He's a bellhop in the Deluxe.'

'I'll find him.'

Hammer closed the door and started back to the stairs. A smile came to his face as he made his way down the bare steps.

SEVEN

Not one single soul within Dodge City realized that the prosperous lawyer who occupied the ground floor building on the main thoroughfare was in fact far more crooked and corrupt than any of the criminals he had defended over the years. His links with the unsavoury outlaws who roamed the vast West went back thirty years. Few men had prospered more that Mason Dwire due to his knowledge of the shady side of life. During those intervening years he had established himself as the most righteous man ever to have set foot in the fledgling settlement known as Dodge City. He had been there when the steel rail tracks from the east had joined up with those from the west. He was a pillar of respectability whose image bore no resemblance to the man himself.

Yet Dwire was a crook through and through. He

was like a rotten chunk of lumber painted with a glossy surface. It fooled everyone except those who knew him.

Sat behind his mahogany desk, Dwire glanced up as he heard the outer door of his large main street office hastily opened and raised voices. The rotund Dwire sat back and rested his shoulders against the padded leather seat in anticipation of the men he had secretly sent for. His baggy eyes stared at his door and waited as the sound of jangling spurs filled the confines of his well-appointed inner sanctum.

Dwire could tell that the spurs which echoed around his second floor office were not those of just one man. They were the combined noise of striding made by at least a half dozen trail-hardened men.

His secretary vainly attempted to stop the progress of his visitors. Dwire placed a cigar between his lips and struck a match across his boot leather. As he sucked in the flame he watched the door open and six dust-caked men stride into his wood-panelled office to the dismay of his hapless secretary.

'You can't just barge in like this,' the weasel-like secretary said as Bart Gibbs pushed him aside and trailed the wide-shouldered Holt into the middle of the office. 'You have to have an appointment. Do you have an appointment?'

Slim Jones stopped and turned. His brutal stare

focused on the fragile Jonas Peters as his hand rested on the grip of his holstered .45.

'You're plumb irritating me,' he growled.

Dwire snapped his fingers at his secretary.

'That's OK, Peters,' Dwire said from behind the cloud of cigar smoke which surrounded him. He waved his hand at the wiry man and ushered him away. 'I'm expecting these gentlemen.'

Emmett Holt pushed the brim of his hat back until it rested on the crown of his head. He cast his deathly eyes at the small Peters and growled, 'You heard your boss, amigo. Beat it. We got business to discuss.'

The feeble Peters grabbed the doorknob and nodded to the men gathered between himself and his employer. He backed away from the six men in dust coats and pulled the door after him.

The sound of the door closing filled the large room. The six wanted men were left standing around the desk looking down at the smiling Dwire.

Holt moved to the desk, placed a hip upon its edge and opened the silver cigar box set to the right of the ink blotter. He lifted its lid and then one of the fat Havana cigars from its gilt interior. The outlaw sniffed it before biting off its tip and spitting it at the floor.

'Help yourself, Emmett,' Dwire said.

'I always do, Mason,' Holt said dryly. 'You know that.'

'I surely do.' The lawyer nodded.

'You sent for me, Mason,' Holt reminded the fat man before picking up a match and igniting it with his thumbnail. 'This job better be good. I've come a long way and I ain't in the mood for anything less than profitable.'

'It's good, Emmett.' Dwire exhaled smoke at the brown ceiling. 'Damn good and very profitable.'

'How good exactly?' Smoke drifted from around Holt's head as he carefully puffed until satisfied the long length of tobacco was alight.

Dwire lowered the cigar from his lips and smiled at the deadly Holt perched on the edge of his desk. It was a sickly smile that had no humour in it. He sat forward on his well-padded chair and looked at the outlaw and his underlings.

'The Cattleman Club,' the rotund man muttered as his eyebrows rose. 'You've heard of it, ain't you?'

Holt nodded his head. 'Sure I've heard of it, Mason. What about it?'

'I ain't stealing no cows,' Bud Collins piped up. 'I don't like cows. They're dangerous.'

Every eye glanced at the outlaw in amusement.

'I can assure you that my friend Mason wouldn't bring me halfway across the country to become a cattle rustler, Bud,' Holt sneered before glancing at Dwire. 'It's more than his life's worth.'

60

Dwire rose to his feet and started to wander around the heavily armed men who had accompanied Holt into his private office. His eyes studied each and every one of them before he reached the side of Holt. Dwire paused and stared straight into the unsmiling face of the lethal outlaw.

'I don't need cattle rustlers. I need you and your hand-picked boys, Emmett,' the rotund man said.

Holt sucked in smoke. 'I'm starting to get interested, Mason. Damn interested. Keep talking.'

The well-established lawyer knew that his reputation meant nothing to any of the six men who were shedding trail dust over his stained floorboards. All they were interested in was a fat payday in recompense for the long journey to Dodge.

'Being in a position of privilege in Dodge and a member of the Cattleman Association I happen to know a few things which most folks don't, Emmett,' Dwire sighed before returning the cigar to his lips briefly and filling his lungs with more smoke. 'I know that the cattle buyers from back east have to place substantial sums of money in the club before they can do their deals with the individual trail drive bosses.'

Emmett Holt raised an eyebrow. 'But the money has already bin paid out, ain't it? Soon as they clinch a deal they hand over the cash.'

61

Dwire shook his head and proceeded to his window. He looked down at the main street for a while and then turned back to Holt.

'Wrong,' he corrected. 'That's the way it seems but that's not the way it's done, Emmett.'

Holt was intrigued. 'Then how's it done?'

Dwire returned to his chair and sat down. 'All of the cattle buyers' agents have to place their money in the Cattleman Club for safe keeping until the herds arrive. Then the agents head on out to the stock pens down at the railhead. They bid against one another until the trail boss agrees a price with one of them. The agent hands a chit to the trail boss and he goes to the club and gets the chit turned into cash. The agents who fail to clinch a deal still have their money with the Cattleman Club.'

The tall figure of Holt stood and started to nod. 'I get it, Mason. The rest of the cash is still in the Cattleman Club until the next herd arrives.'

'Now you got it.' Dwire pointed a finger at the outlaw and chuckled. 'There are eight buyers in Dodge City right now waiting for herds to arrive. Every one of the bastards has deposited small fortunes in the Cattleman Club to cover their bids for herds that have yet to come into Dodge. That's an awful lot of cash, Emmett.'

Holt stared at the man before him. Dwire was one

of the most respected men in the settlement but he was as crooked as any of the outlaws who rode with Holt. In all the years he had known the lawyer he had yet to hear him either lie or exaggerate when it came to hard cash.

'That's a fortune, Mason,' he sneered before taking a long thoughtful pull on his cigar. As the smoke filled his lungs he began to nod knowingly. 'We ain't no safe crackers but I got me a feeling that we won't have to be. Am I right?'

'Damn right,' Dwire chuckled before pointing at the five men standing behind Holt. 'Are these boys good?'

'The best.' Holt grinned.

Dwire swung his chair around and rested his elbows on the ink blotter as he tapped the ash from his cigar into the already full ashtray. 'I know the Cattleman Club like the back of my hand. I can give you an exact route to the safe and I even have the combination.'

'How'd you get that?' Holt asked as he leaned across the desk and patted his cigar over the tray. 'You didn't steal it, did you?'

Dwire shook his head. 'I didn't have to, Emmett. I hold the insurance policy on the club. For a substantial fee I was given the combination to the safe when it was installed.'

'He's as crooked as us,' Bud Collins quipped, pointing at Dwire.

The leader of the gang gazed in Collins' direction. 'Wrong, Bud. He's far worse than we could ever hope to be. Old Mason here is a lawyer.'

'Lawyers are the worst kind of crooks,' Gibbs grinned.

Ignoring the complimentary insults, Dwire looked up at Holt and pointed his cigar at him.

'Let's get down to business, Emmett.' Dwire opened a desk drawer and produced a bottle of amber liquor. He placed it on the desk and then pointed at a stack of glasses on a sideboard. 'You all look like you could use some whiskey and this is twelve-year-old double malt. I have it imported for special occasions.'

The outlaws gathered seven glasses and placed them down on the blotter as Dwire broke the seal on the whiskey bottle and pulled its cork. He poured the aromatic liquor into the glasses and watched as the outlaws lifted them up one by one.

'When do you want the job done, Mason?' Holt asked.

Dwire sipped at the whiskey and then leaned back. His watery eyes stared at them as he returned the cigar to his lips.

'Tonight,' he said firmly.

Holt nodded and downed his liquor. 'I was thinking, surely your fellow members of the club will figure that you must have something to do with the robbery, Mason. You having the combination to the safe and all. It stands to reason that they'll know that you must have had something to do with it.'

'They do not know of my purchasing the combination to their safe, Emmett,' Dwire informed him. 'That was a private piece of business between myself and the gentleman who installed the safe.'

'Damn, you are slick.' Holt grinned.

Dwire smiled. 'There's a train leaving Dodge at exactly midnight and I intend being on that train. I've already purchased the ticket. By the time the club figures out that they've been robbed I'll be hundreds of miles away.'

'How much do you figure your share should be, Mason?' Holt filled their glasses again.

'Fifty per cent,' the fat man replied.

'Half?' Slim Jones queried. 'That's a hell of a lot, ain't it?'

'It sure is,' Dwire agreed. 'But without my knowledge you boys would not be able to get close enough to that safe and its contents. Besides, after this job we can all retire for good. You have no idea how much is in the club safe right now.'

'How much is there in the safe, Mason?' Holt

growled as he downed the fiery liquor and stared down at the unnervingly calm lawyer. 'It better be a lot if you're figuring on taking half.'

Unabashed, Dwire sat forward and pulled a pencil from his vest pocket. He scribbled on a notebook, tore the sheet of paper free and then turned it around so that they all could see the huge sum he had just written down.

'Is this a large enough figure, Emmett?' he asked.

A mutual gasp went around the desk as Holt showed his five hirelings what the lawyer had scribbled.

'I never figured that there was that much money in the whole country,' Dante sighed.

A wide smile encompassed the face of Mason Dwire as he drew smoke into his lungs and then lowered the glowing cigar back to the ashtray.

'There's more,' he chuckled with amusement. 'The entire contents of the bank is also being stored in the Cattleman safe at the moment.'

Holt looked down upon the crooked lawyer. 'How come?'

'The bank was originally constructed out of wood like most of the other places in Dodge,' Dwire informed his eager audience. 'That was fine when the bank was put up but not anymore. The stock holders decided at a meeting a couple of weeks back that it was far safer to put the bank's cash in the brick and stone Cattleman Club until they can have the bank strengthened.'

'How'd you know this, Mason?' Gibbs asked.

'I happen to be a major stock holder at the bank.' Dwire smiled. 'I was the one who started to get troubled by the bank's meagre defences against being robbed. Like I told them, anyone with a crowbar could bust into the bank. It was far safer in the Cattleman Club safe.'

Holt laughed out loud. 'You sure are a tricky varmint, Mason. Tricky and slick.'

'So you will not only have all the cattle agents' loot to steal but the bank's as well.' The rotund man sat back in his padded chair and sucked hard on his cigar.

Collins rubbed his unshaven jaw. 'That's a lot of money, boys. How the hell are we gonna get all that cash out of Dodge without being caught?'

'It can't be done,' Harper frowned.

Gibbs grabbed Holt's arm. 'The boys are right, Emmett. That's more cash than we could ever carry out of town. We'll need a wagon and that's a darn slow way of making a getaway. We'll get slaughtered before we get to the range.'

Holt stared with cold eyes at his seated paymaster. 'My boys are right, Mason. How the hell are we meant to get that much cash away from this town without being caught?'

'I've already thought about that, Emmett,' the lawyer retorted through cigar smoke. 'I figured that three coffins ought to be just the right size to hold most of the money. You leave the small bills and coinage where it is and only take the larger denomination bills.'

Holt leaned closer to the legal eagle.

'Where the hell are we gonna get hold of three coffins, Mason?' he asked.

'I've already purchased three coffins,' Dwire said. 'Three metal coffins arrived last week from Chicago. They're still boxed and stacked in my warehouse. I also have a small wagon for transportation.'

'Warehouse?' Holt repeated. 'Since when have you had a warehouse, Mason?'

'Since a vacant building came on to the market,' Dwire answered drily as he lifted his glass and drank its fiery contents. 'The structure is directly behind the Cattleman Club.'

'That's handy,' Dante sighed.

'You must be one hell of a lawyer,' Gibbs grinned. 'You think of everything in advance.'

Holt straightened up to his full imposing height. 'He is one hell of a lawyer, boys. Old Mason thinks a hundred yards ahead of everyone else. Always has.'

'Once you have filled the coffins and bolted them down you will take them to the railhead and have them placed in the guard's van. I will accompany the coffins in a private car I have arranged to be added to the cattle cars. The railroad will escort our precious cargo and you can then ride out of Dodge free and clear,' Dwire informed his six listeners.

Emmett Holt stared at his refilled glass of whiskey and considered the job they were about to undertake. Everything seemed to have been planned to perfection by the fat lawyer who wallowed in his own devious brilliance. Everything apart from one small detail. One which Emmett Holt would keep close to his chest until the time was right to present it to the smug, overweight lawyer.

'Fifty per cent of that sum is agreeable, Mason,' he drawled and pointed at the notepad. 'Now start drawing us a plan of the Cattleman Club and the combination to its safe. We don't want to make no mistakes.'

'How many folks do you reckon we'll have to kill?' Gibbs asked as he swallowed the contents of his tumbler.

'For that amount of money I'd kill every damn critter in Dodge City, Bart,' Holt snarled as he watched the lawyer sketching out a floorplan of the club.

Dwire looked up from the notebook he was working on.

'With any luck you'll not have to kill anyone, boys,' he said. 'In fact, it would be better if you didn't. By the time they realize that there's been a robbery, we'll all be gone.'

Holt rested his hip back on the edge of the desk. He stared at the amber liquid in his glass and ventured, 'How much time have we got?'

'The train will leave Dodge just before midnight,' Dwire said knowingly. 'More than enough time for you to load the coffins and be long gone, Emmett.'

'Keep scribbling, Mason,' he said before glancing over his shoulder at the office door. He thought about the weedy man in the outer office and then returned his attention to the lawyer as he drew on the large pad.

'Where are we gonna meet up to split the loot?' Gibbs wondered as he watched the lawyer carefully drawing.

Holt leaned over Dwire's shoulder.

'Bart's got a point, Mason,' he whispered. 'Where are we gonna meet up to divide the loot?'

Dwire paused. 'I'll tell you that after you deliver the three coffins to the train down at the stockyard.'

Holt rubbed the nape of his neck. He knew that his original idea of killing both Dwire and the mild-mannered secretary would have to wait a while.

'Hell, you're even smarter that I figured, Mason,' he sighed.

Dwire glanced at Holt knowingly. 'Damn right I am.'

EIGHT

A large white-faced clock chimed yet few of the sweating men who toiled beneath the relentless sun heard any of the nine bells which rang out from its weathered carcass. The stock pens were being readied for the next arrival of prime Texan steers, which were due within the next few days. Half of the herd which Tom McGee had expertly delivered to the famed Dodge City yards were still awaiting transportation by the next train to wind its way into the heart of the railhead.

Tough men of all shapes and sizes went about their daily rituals as expertly as those with far more profitable and acceptable professions. They knew how to handle even the most brutish of steers and how to get them from one stock pen to another and entice them up into the stock cars.

The pair of lawmen had entered the vastly different end of town toting their weaponry with trepidation. There was little if any respect for star packers in and around the aromatic stockyards. They lived and died by a different set of rules to those who dwelled in the better side of the cattle town. They tended to sort out their own troubles without any help from men like Marshal Cole Grey and his deputy Ben Graff.

'Keep your wits primed, boy,' Grey said through gritted teeth, the pungent smell growing stronger as they ventured deeper into the confines of the yards. Both men knew that if they got into any trouble in this part of Dodge, they could not depend on any help coming from the rest of town. They were on their own and they both knew it.

'Why the hell do we have to come down here, Marshal?' Graff asked as his sweating hands gripped his scattergun tightly. 'They sure don't want us poking our noses into their business.'

The middle-aged marshal nodded as they strode along the wooden platforms and stared at the rail tracks gleaming in the morning sun.

'It's part of our duties, Ben,' Grey replied. 'We gotta come down here once a day to earn our pay. Them's the rules.'

The skittish Graff licked his dry lips as his eyes

darted around them at the faces of the men who toiled in this cesspit of a place.

'Even if there was trouble around here, we sure couldn't do much about it,' the deputy grumbled.

'You never said a truer word, boy,' Grey sighed. 'You'd need an army to make these hombres obey the rules. Even if you arrest one of them it don't make it any easier. The last marshal to do so got himself killed a short while after his office was raised to the ground. They stick together down here.'

'But we still gotta come down here?' Graff gulped. 'I got the feeling that there's a gun aimed at me with every step we take.'

'That's 'coz there is.' Cole Grey glanced at his partner. 'As long as they don't start squeezing them triggers, we'll be OK.'

The two men continued to do their rounds. A job neither they nor the countless sweat-soaked men who observed them liked.

Dust floated up into the blue sky as pen gates were closed along the tracks. The huge ramps were raised and pinned back up to secure the moaning cattle inside the cattle cars. A huge black cloud of smoke exploded up into the sky as the mighty engine started to move.

The massive locomotive full of cattle had no sooner left the stockyards than another equally large train pulling a long caravan of empty cars behind its tender hissed its way into Dodge City and wound its way across the rail points to where it would take the remainder of the large herd Tom McGee had auctioned hours earlier.

Both lawmen watched as men emerged from every shadow and began the process all over again.

'Them hombres sure know what they gotta do,' Graff noted as he dried his temple on the back of his sleeve. 'Look at them, Marshal. They're like a swarm of ants.'

'They know their jobs OK,' Grey agreed.

The stock pens covered an area beside the tracks even larger than the sprawling town itself and over the previous few months had seldom been empty. Herds were making their way from at least a dozen starting points to be sent back east. Dodge had never been so busy or so dangerous.

Both Marshal Cole Grey and his newly appointed deputy Ben Graff realized it. The lawmen carried their scatterguns across their chests and moved through the grim yards as fast as their boots would carry them. They would not reduce their pace until they were back in the heart of Dodge itself.

They stared at the large locomotive as it sent black smoke signals up from its tall stack. The whistle began to summon the mysterious figures to it.

75

'Look at them, Marshal,' Graff said as they approached the far side of the vast stockyards. 'They're like moths to a flame. Where in tarnation do they all come from?'

'It's best we don't know where them hombres come from, Ben,' Grey groaned as he continued to peel his eyes and watch every shadow. The sun was blinding and they were headed directly toward it as it slowly rose above the numerous wooden shacks and warehouses that dominated the yard. 'We just walk through here like we're paid to do and keep on walking until we get back to civilization.'

Although neither had ever had the misfortune of encountering trouble at the railhead, they knew that anything could happen in this part of town. If it did, they wanted nothing to do with it.

Both men skipped across rail tracks and headed up to where they could at last see the way out of the yard. Beads of sweat rolled down from their hatbands as they passed the juggernaut of a locomotive, hissing like a thousand ornery rattlers. Jets of boiling steam shot from behind its wheels and kicked up even more dust than the moaning white-faced cattle could muster.

Grey looked at the pens to their left. There were at least a thousand steers still remaining to be transported to the insatiable eastern seaboard. Men with long prodding poles somehow defied gravity and ran across the top of the wooden pens jabbing at the stubborn animals. Slowly but surely the steers began to move toward the train through their man-made avenues.

'I sure wouldn't wanna be one of them steers, Marshal,' Graff said as they kept walking to the way out of this noisy and dangerous place.

'They'll be sizzling on a fancy plate in a couple of days, boy,' Grey thought as he rubbed his throat and licked his lips. 'Damn I'm hungry.'

The marshal paused as they stepped up on to the high platform. Graff stopped beside his superior and clutched his shotgun across his belly as Grey squinted over the countless pens. Steam rose from the cattle, which were still contained in their temporary holding pens.

'What's wrong, Marshal?' Graff asked as the older man bit his lower lip and continued to survey the sun-bleached area below their high vantage point.

Grey glanced at his deputy. 'There ain't nothing wrong, Ben. I've just got me a feeling in my innards that something ain't right, that's all.'

The deputy stepped closer to his mentor. 'You got a gut feeling that there might be trouble brewing?'

'Yep.' Marshal Grey nodded and stared across at the numerous men who were moving between the pens. Some were watering the steers and others were feeding the anxious cattle. 'Something's gnawing at my craw besides the fact that I ain't had no breakfast.'

'What we gonna do about it?' The deputy paced around his stationary boss. His young eyes darted between every man in the area. Just like the marshal, Graff knew that this was another world compared to the rest of Dodge. They lived by different rules in this part of town. Men lived and died here from various causes and yet news of any tragedies seldom reached the ears of the lawmen.

'Nothing, Ben,' Grey replied. 'We stay out of it whatever it might be. I got a hankering to try and live long enough to earn my pension.'

The naïve deputy stared at Grey. 'We ain't gonna do nothing at all?'

The marshal patted his deputy on the shoulder. 'There's enough trouble brewing in all the whore houses and saloons down yonder, Ben. That's more than we can handle if the truth were known.'

The youngster dried his temple again.

'So they can do whatever they like around here without us getting tangled up in it?' he gasped.

Grey nodded. 'Yep. The only time we get involved is if they start shooting in our direction, boy. Otherwise we don't see or hear nothing. Savvy?'

Graff shrugged. 'I reckon so.'

'These bastards got enough troubles without the law adding to their burden, Ben.' The marshal rested the twin-barrelled scattergun on his shoulder and turned away from the huge train.

Graff sniffed and then rubbed his nose in a vain bid to rid the smell of manure away. 'I reckon you're right, Marshal. This place gotta be the worst place anyone could wish to find themselves in.'

The marshal started to lead his deputy on the last leg of their journey through the maze of pens, wide-eyed steers snorting and grunting as they became dimly aware that their plight was far from over.

'Even the cowboys that bring the steers in here don't loiter too long,' Grey drawled. 'And most cow-punchers ain't the brightest candles in the box but they're smart enough to know that this part of town is damn lethal.'

Graff nodded and trailed his boss as the sturdy marshal stared at the train coming to a halt two hundred yards away from the platform they were standing upon.

'That locomotive must be intending picking up passengers, Marshal,' The deputy said.

'What makes you say that, Ben?' Grey asked.

The deputy aimed the barrel of his weapon at the passenger car being tagged on to the end of the long line of cattle cars.

'Look, Marshal,' Graff urged.

Grey looked and paused for a moment. The well-appointed Pullman car looked out of place. 'At least it'll be downwind of these white-faced steers.'

The constant wailing of cattle sent a chill down the spines of both men. They glanced at one another and then the elder of the lawmen curled his finger at the deputy.

'C'mon, boy. Let's get the hell out of here and get some grub,' he said before turning and marching away from the train. 'The sound of steers kicking up a fuss like that spooks me something awful.'

The two men walked shoulder to shoulder.

'Do you think them steers know what's going to happen to them, Marshal?' Graff asked as he glanced over his shoulder and squinted through the haze and the dust.

'They know, boy,' Grey sighed. 'They know.'

NINE

The Cheyenne cowboy glanced through the steam which rose from his coffee cup and noticed the two lawmen had just entered the main street. He lifted his spoon and was about to stir the black beverage when he saw the green blinds being lifted on the bank's doors. Within seconds the door was opened and a few of the locals were allowed to enter.

'Is everything OK, Cheyenne?' a gentle voice asked from behind Hammer's left shoulder. 'You confused?'

Hammer glanced at the buxom waitress and smiled. 'I am a little confused, ma'am.'

She moved around the table top where they could look straight at one another.

'What you confused about?' she pressed.

He lifted a finger and pointed at the two men

striding down the long street opposite his position by the window of the small café. The sun glinted off their tin stars like dazzling fireflies.

'Who the hell are they?' Hammer wondered loudly. 'They sure ain't the same lawmen that were here six months ago.'

'That's Marshal Grey and his new deputy,' the waitress answered before placing his dessert down beside his hand.

'Earp's gone?' Hammer asked.

'They say old Wyatt and his kin are headed for Tombstone,' she ventured. 'Must be some real big money over there if the Earps are interested.'

Hammer lifted the cup, downed the coffee and then placed it back down upon its saucer. He rose and adjusted his gun belt. She watched as the wide-shouldered young cowboy moved toward the door. She was about to speak when he interrupted her before any words could escape from her crimson lips.

'I'll be back for that handsome looking slice of pie, ma'am.' He smiled and pulled the door toward him.

'I keep telling you that my name's Betsy, Cheyenne,' she sighed. 'When are you gonna start calling me by my name?'

'I'll be back, Betsy,' he said as he stepped out on to the boardwalk.

The mature female exhaled loudly as she watched the handsome cowboy walking toward the bank. Her eyelashes fluttered to the pounding of her heart.

'If only I was five years younger,' she regretted.

Hammer touched his hat brim as he crossed paths with the lawmen.

'Marshal,' he acknowledged.

Grey returned the greeting. 'Cheyenne.'

The cowboy stepped up on to the bank's boardwalk and looked at the two lawmen as they continued on their way toward their office at the far end of town. He was still perplexed that everyone in Dodge seemed to know him by name. In his opinion his brief and bloody encounter with Emmett Holt and his previous band of followers must have been greatly exaggerated by the newspapers. Hammer knew the truth; he had gotten lucky and his bumping into the ruthless outlaws had been purely accidental.

The cowboy recalled how it seemed that every shot he had fired that day, had somehow found its mark. What had appeared to be skill had been nothing more than luck.

Then as he turned and entered the bank, he was greeted by the rosy-cheeked man he recognized as the owner. The man beamed and rushed toward the cowboy with open arms.

'Cheyenne, my boy.' Farnum Foster greeted Hammer loudly and wrapped his arms around the cowboy. 'I guess you're here to collect your reward money.'

'My what?' Hammer stared down at the far shorter Foster in utter surprise. 'What reward money?'

'As if you didn't know.' Foster released his grip and patted the cowboy on his back before leading him to his private office. 'I have it all ready for you.'

Hammer frowned. 'You have?'

'I certainly have.' Foster nodded like a dog with ticks. 'I'm not going to mess with the famed Cheyenne cowboy.'

The door closed behind the confused cowboy and Hammer found himself turning full circle as his eyes trailed the excited Foster around the interior of his office.

'What's going on, Mr Foster?' Hammer asked.

'Sit down, Cheyenne.' The owner of the bank gestured at the chair across the desk from his own far grander seat. As the cowboy sat down Foster opened his desk and produced a telegraph message. He showed it to Hammer. 'You earned some rather big money by your actions, my boy. I've been contacted by the authorities down south to pay you three thousand dollars' bounty. It seems you rejoined the cattle drive before they could pay you themselves.'

The cowboy felt his jaw drop at the unexpected news.

'I'm being paid for getting mixed up with them outlaws?' he gulped in surprise. 'Hell, I only done what any other hombre would have done.'

'Modesty.' Foster smiled as he withdrew a pile of cash from the drawer and started counting it out on the ink blotter before him. 'I like that. Modesty.'

Hammer stared at the cash on the desk and swallowed hard as the skilful hands of the banker shuffled it into a neat stack. He rubbed his jaw.

'Those critters were worth money dead or alive?' he asked. 'And just coz I killed them, I'm being paid?'

Foster handed the cash to Hammer. 'Indeed you are. This is payment by grateful authorities. I am proud to hand it to you, my boy.'

Hammer looked up at the joyous Foster.

'But I came here to put money into my account, Mr Foster,' he said drily. 'I'm a tad mixed up.'

'I read all about your exploits in the newspaper, Cheyenne.' Foster nodded frantically. 'Such bravery. You must be one of the fastest men with a six-shooter in the territory.'

'I just got lucky,' Hammer tried to explain.

'There's no need to be modest here, my boy.' Foster smiled as he sat on the edge of his desk and stared at the dumbfounded cowboy. 'We've all read the newspaper reports of the incident.'

Hammer pulled out his bank book and trail drive earnings and piled it together with his newly acquired fortune. He sheepishly handed it all to Foster.

'Can I deposit this with you, sir?' he asked nervously.

Foster snatched it out of the cowboy's hands. A wide smile crossed the face of the rosy-cheeked banker. 'Of course you can.'

Within seconds the banker had jotted down the details in Hammer's bank book and returned it to the cowboy. He then led the still-befuddled youngster back to his office door and out to the street. Both men paused on the boardwalk as Foster looked the cowboy up and down as though inspecting him.

'What are you intending to do with all that money, Cheyenne?' he asked the cowboy who was staring down at the bank book in his hands.

'I'm gonna look for a small ranch in these parts soon, Mr Foster,' Hammer explained as he slid the book into the safety of his shirt pocket. 'Reckon I got more than enough now.'

'You surely have, Cheyenne.' The banker grinned. 'What are you gonna do now?'

'I reckon I'll go eat me some pie,' Hammer said as

he stared at the café and the well-endowed female in the café window. Then the cowboy looked to where Foster had been standing on the boardwalk next to him and realized that the banker had gone back into his office. 'Yep, I'm gonna go eat that pie.'

The agile young cowboy hopped down on to the sandy street and started to walk toward the café. His mind was racing with the possibilities that were now open to him with an extra three thousand bucks to his name. Two handsome females crossed before him and glanced in his direction. He smiled, touched his hat brim and they giggled. He watched as they hurried on their way holding their parasols aloft against the merciless sun.

Grinning, Hammer continued toward the smell of freshly baked apple pie. He was halfway across the wide thoroughfare when his attention was drawn to the sound of jangling spurs coming from down the street.

The noise of the spurs seemed familiar.

When the Cheyenne cowboy reached the opposite side of the street he stepped up on to the boardwalk. He rested a shoulder against a porch upright and stared into the bright, sunbathed street to where the sound of the spurs still chimed. Few men wore spurs that rang out. Most preferred the silent type he and his fellow cowboys favoured.

His eyes narrowed.

Hammer watched silently as the six figures left the lawyer's office and walked in single file across the wide street. They looked even dirtier than when he had first noticed their arrival in Dodge from his hotel window.

The jangling spurs nagged at his mind. He had heard something like it before but could not recall where or when. The cowboy stroked his throat thoughtfully as he studied the men still clad in their long dust coats and listened to their spurs ringing out.

It was like the tolling of deathly bells.

'Who the hell are those critters?' he whispered low and quietly as he continued to observe them. 'They sure don't look like they're here to start quoting from the scriptures.'

Curiosity still nagged at Hammer's craw. He knew that men who looked the way those men looked usually rode on the wrong side of the law. Their long dust coats reached down to their boots and hid a multitude of sins from eagle-eyed onlookers.

Had Hammer been closer to them he might have recognized Emmett Holt as the man he had bested months earlier. Yet the shimmering heat haze and distance made it impossible for him to see any of their faces clearly.

Then his eyebrows rose as he noticed where they were heading. The town was full of whore houses of various shapes and sizes but the most famous of them all was the China Doll. It was reputed to be the first permanent structure to be erected in Dodge after the barber had laid claim to the prime site. The China Doll was different to all of its competitors and boasted to have nothing but beautiful oriental females within its four walls.

That was where the jangling spurs were heading toward, Hammer noted with a blushing smile. Maybe his suspicions were ill-founded. Maybe all the riders had were burning desires to scratch an itch.

As the six figures disappeared into the China Doll, Hammer turned and entered the café again. He resumed his place at the window table and hung his hat on his holstered .45.

The cowboy did not know it but the man who led his five followers into the China Doll was the very same man who had tried to kill him months earlier when Hammer had innocently found himself in the middle of a blazing gun battle.

'Pie, Cheyenne honey?' Betsy asked him from the café counter.

He glanced over his shoulder and nodded. As the well-rounded female placed the small plate with the generous portion of apple pie upon its blue design, his mind flashed with memories yet he still did not connect the mysterious leader of the newly arrived riders with the bloody fight months earlier.

'Is it OK, Cheyenne?' the female asked pointing at the apple pie.

'If it tastes half as good as it looks, it'll be great, ma'am.' Hammer picked up the fork and then paused as more thoughts filled his already confused mind.

He wondered why everyone seemed to be calling him by his nickname of Cheyenne. They had never done that before in Dodge, he thought. Then it started to dawn on him.

The banker had mentioned the gunfight before presenting him with the bounty money. The bellhop over in the Deluxe Hotel had also made it obvious that he had read about not only the incident but also about him. Hammer remembered that the newspaper men had asked him several questions after the carnage when Holt had made his escape.

Hammer recalled that he had told the eager journalists after the deadly gunfight that he was from Cheyenne and was a cowboy taking a herd to Dodge. He had not read any of their writings because he had to return to the cattle drive.

'Hey, Betsy,' he said as he slid the fork through the mouth-watering pie. 'Did you read about me in the local newspapers a few months back?'

'I sure did.' She nodded. 'You were front-page news, Cheyenne. They made you sound like Wild Bill Hickok. Didn't you read any of the stories?'

'Nope, I've bin kinda busy bringing a herd of steers to market, ma'am.' Hammer chewed the pie thoughtfully. Finally he began to put two and two together. The journalists must have turned him into some sort of hero and manufactured the fight into a valiant and heroic act. 'I ain't seen a newspaper in months.'

'You sure must be brave, Cheyenne.' She smiled widely and walked back to her counter. 'Probably the bravest man ever to eat my pie.'

'A varmint don't have to be brave to eat your pie.' Hammer smiled as he devoured the pie. 'Even a yellow belly could manage the job.'

Betsy was not listening. She opened the door of her stove and pulled out a tray with even more fragrant pies upon it.

'Did you say something, Cheyenne honey?' Betsy wondered from the rear of the café.

A wry smile etched his face as he swallowed the pie and carved another mouthful out with his fork. He turned his head and looked at Betsy.

'This is the best apple pie I've ever tasted, ma'am,' he laughed. 'Delicious. Real delicious.'

91

'Keep eating,' Betsy chuckled as she watched the young man with more than a little interest. 'It might just put some hair on your chest, Cheyenne.'

He nodded in agreement. Hair on his chest would at least be a start and once there they might even spread up to his face, he thought.

'Will you bring me another slice of mighty fine pie please, Betsy?' he asked as his fork scraped the plate in search of its last remnants.

The female cut another portion of the pie and carefully placed it on to a small plate. 'You want some coffee to wash it down?'

Hammer raised an eyebrow. 'I'd be obliged, Betsy.'

The friendly female walked to the table and placed the plate before him. She then placed the coffee mug beside it and put a hand on his shoulder.

'Anything else you want, Cheyenne?' she purred like a large kitten. 'Anything at all?'

'No thanks.' He naïvely smiled and picked up his fork. 'This'll be fine, Betsy.'

'I was afraid of that.' She exhaled and walked away from the window table.

Hammer stared out into the bright street as horses and other forms of transport passed. Then he remembered the jangling spurs that had attracted his attention. He rubbed his smooth chin and thought about Holt again.

TEN

Darkness had come swiftly to Dodge City. Less than thirty minutes after the blazing sun had set the entire town was bathed in the eerie hue of night. At one time this was a subtle signal for terrified men to huddle together in caves for fear of encountering the nocturnal creatures that roamed after sundown in search of their prey.

Yet few of the thousands of folks in Dodge even noticed the transition from day to night. Theirs was a well-rehearsed acceptance of the inevitable and each knew how to welcome the coming of sundown without fearing it. Every street lantern was lit and the majority of store fronts spilled lamplight across the sandy streets. Dodge City was said to be one of those rare places in the Wild West where some people did not sleep. Poker games had been known to go on for weeks or even longer. But even though fear had been replaced by apathy there was still good reason for the people of Dodge to be wary of night.

For death awaited the unwary in the shadows which even coal-tar lantern light could not penetrate. Dodge City defiantly glowed like a beacon in an otherwise dark land and lured the good and the bad alike into its web of endless intrigue.

Farnum Foster locked the door of his bank as a team of muscular stonemasons began unloading their wagon in preparation for the night's work. The banker watched as the men unloaded blocks of masonry to add to the building's walls.

He quickened his pace and encouraged the pair of heavily laden clerks on toward the Cattleman Club. 'Hurry up, boys. The quicker we get this money to the club the quicker you can go home.'

The bank clerks carried the day's takings across the street toward the Cattleman Club. They walked down the dimly lit alley to the rear door of the club. At the rear entrance the chairman of the club ushered them into the structure's ornate interior and along a corridor to where the huge safe stood between two pillars.

The bank employees placed the bank takings into the safe and watched as Silas Chester locked the five-foot high safe back up. Foster patted the clerks on their backs.

'That's fine, boys,' Foster told them. 'You get off home now. Be here at nine in the morning.'

The young men nodded and left before the banker thought of something else for them to do.

'You trust them young 'uns?' Chester asked the banker as they began to retrace their steps back to the alley.

'Sure do, Chester,' Foster replied. 'They're kin.'

Upon reaching the alley Farnum Foster accepted the receipt from his old pal and placed it into his bill-fold. The banker paused as Chester locked the side metal door. They strolled back toward the amber illuminated main street and stopped to look at the bank. The stone-block walls were already half built.

'When will the reconstruction of the bank be completed, Foster?' Silas Chester asked the banker. 'I reckon that will be the best bank in the territory by the time it's finished.'

Foster looked at the chairman of the Cattleman Club and shrugged as he slid the billfold back into his deep pocket.

'They estimated it will take a month. It can't be soon enough for me though, Silas.' He sighed as he watched Chester resting his knuckles on his wide hips. 'This is most bothersome having to bring the day's takings over here every day for safe-keeping.

Having to depend on the Cattleman Club makes me nervous.'

'It'll be worth it,' Chester smiled.

'I know but it makes me nervous having to cross the street with all that cash, Silas,' Foster admitted.

Wanting to take Foster's mind off his precious bank, Chester rested a hand on the shorter man's shoulder as they walked down through the strange amber light that cascaded from all sides on the long thoroughfare.

'You need to take your mind off it, Foster.'

The banker nodded. 'I'll admit that it is wearing me down, Silas old friend.'

Chester clapped his hands together.

'Listen up. I hear they've got a fresh shipment of Scottish double malt whisky down in the Long Branch saloon, Farnum,' he informed his friend enthusiastically.

Foster suddenly looked less concerned as he stared up at his taller friend. He rubbed his mouth and then licked his lips.

'Real Scottish whisky?' he questioned. 'Genuine real imported Scottish whisky?'

'That's what I'm told, Farnum.' Chester tucked his thumbs in his vest pockets. 'We could go and sample a few drams if you're willing.'

'Then what are we waiting for?' Foster grabbed

Chester's arm and started walking at pace in the direction of the town's largest saloon. 'Lead the way.'

A lace drape was pulled aside in one of the second storey windows of the China Doll. As female hands clawed at him in a vain attempt to drag him back to the still-warm bed, Emmett Holt bit the tip off a cigar and placed the long weed in the corner of his mouth. He scratched a match and raised the flame and sucked. Holt inhaled deeply and then pushed the female aside.

'You've done your business, woman,' Holt snarled before turning and moving to the few bits of clothing he had removed before servicing the attractive lady of the night.

'You go?' The beautiful raven-haired female watched as he swiftly dressed and then buckled his gun belt. 'Why you go? The night is still young. We can have much good time.'

Holt placed his Stetson over his hair and glanced at her as he unbolted the door and pulled it open.

'I've got business, gal,' he sneered before tossing a golden coin into her hands. 'Much obliged.'

The near-naked female moved to the corridor and watched as the tall Holt beat his fist on the adjoining doors and shouted for his men to quit what they were doing.

'I'll wait for you galoots downstairs in the parlour,'

Holt shouted before racing down the steps and entering the dimly illuminated small room. He moved through the over-powering smell of stale perfume and raised a window blind. His eyes narrowed as he sucked more smoke into his lungs and watched the banker and chairman of the Cattleman as they entered the Long Branch saloon.

'Dead on time,' Holt muttered through the smoke, which filtered through what remained of his teeth. 'Old Mason said they'd head to the Long Branch after they put the bank takings in the club safe.'

Holt pulled the blind down to cover the window and then leaned on an upright piano. His bloodthirsty eyes stared at the neatly decorated parlour and the cheap oriental decorations which surrounded him. So far everything the crooked Dwire had told him was correct.

The sound of spurs rang out behind Holt. The lethal hired gunman slowly raised his head up and glanced at them.

Gibbs stopped just short of the outlaw leader.

'Is it time, Emmett?' he asked as he adjusted his hastily buttoned shirt.

Holt glanced at his pocket watch and nodded. 'Things are going exactly the way old Dwire said they would. That hombre is always hot on detail.'

Both men looked to the sound of more spurs as the rest of the gang made their way down to the parlour and started plucking their dust coats off the wall pegs.

'Can we trust that lawyer, Emmett?' Gibbs asked. 'That critter is slimy. I don't trust him.'

'All lawyers are like that, Bart,' Holt said through cigar smoke as he pulled on his own long dust coat. 'He wouldn't try to cross us though. Not for the amount of cash he says is in that safe.'

Gibbs still looked anxious. 'He might be figuring on trying to get the reward money on our heads. Have you thought about that?'

Holt looked around the faces of his men then shook his head. He pulled the cigar from his teeth and tapped its ash on to the threadbare carpet beneath their feet.

'He wouldn't do that, Bart,' the outlaw leader said as he returned the cigar to his mouth and then quickly checked his weapons. 'He's too greedy. The collective price on our heads ain't worth spit compared to the amount of cattle agent money he said was in the club safe. That combined with the takings from the bank add up to a tidy sum. Mason wouldn't dream of crossing us. He knows I'd kill him if he did and he likes being alive way too much.'

Bud Collins watched Holt checking his golden

hunter again and moved toward the far taller man. 'How come you keep looking at your watch, Emmett?'

'Mason told me he'd arrange a buckboard for us to use to get them coffins to the rail tracks, Bud,' Holt hissed like a rattler before sliding the timepiece back into his pocket. 'I figure it'll be arriving in about five minutes.'

The six rough and ready men filed out of the China Doll on to the shadowy boardwalk. Holt raised a hand to his ear as he stood beneath a wall lantern, which was draped in red cloth.

'What's wrong, Emmett?' Dante asked.

Holt indicated to his men. 'Listen up, boys. Do you hear that?'

The noise, which was clearly made by hoofs, wheel rims and chains, grew louder.

'I surely do know what that is,' Gibbs nodded. 'It's a flatbed wagon.'

Holt pulled his hat brim down and nodded as his teeth bit into the cigar. 'Damn right. That's the buckboard old Mason ordered for us if I ain't mistaken.'

'That lawyer thinks of everything.' Wes Harper spat at the boardwalk.

'Luckily for us,' Gibbs sighed.

Above the sound of the boisterous townsfolk the

distinctive noise of a buckboard could be heard as it travelled toward them from the direction of the distant livery stable. The six men watched as the two-horse team pulled the hefty vehicle around the corner and travelled in front of the Long Branch. The burly blacksmith hauled back on the reins and stopped the wagon just as Holt led his five followers toward it from under the dark porch overhang.

'Just like old Mason promised,' Holt grinned. 'A buckboard to help us take the coffins to the railhead. Damn, that old bastard's good.'

The muscular blacksmith looked around the street and then spotted the six men he had encountered hours earlier showered in the red glow of the China Doll. He looped the reins around the brake pole and gestured in Holt's direction.

'Are you the critters expecting this flatbed?' Barker shouted at them as he slowly descended from the driver's board. He clapped the dust from his large hands and squinted at the six men. 'Well, are you?'

'That's right,' Holt nodded.

Clem Barker eyed them up and down. They still did not impress him for he had encountered their breed many times before. Men who lived and usually died by the gun were a pitiful bunch in his mind.

'How long are you critters intending leaving them

horses of yours with me, boys?' The blacksmith stared at them and flexed his many muscles.

'We're leaving tonight, big man,' Holt replied as he chewed on his cigar. 'Get them ready for a long ride when you get back to your stable. We oughta be ready to mosey on out of Dodge in about an hour at most.'

Barker looked slightly confused. He scratched his balding head and screwed up his eyes as he stood toe-to-toe with Holt. He frowned.

'If you boys are intending riding out later, what in tarnation do you want this buckboard for?' he asked the outlaw leader curiously. 'That don't make no sense.'

For a few moments Holt said nothing as he paced around the large man and puffed on his cigar. Then he paused beside one of the sturdy horses and rattled its chains. His eyes darted at the liveryman.

'We're just doing the lawyer a favour, friend,' Holt drawled as he stroked the long neck of the powerful horse.

'You're doing old Mason a favour, huh?' Barker repeated the statement but did not believe a word of it.

'We sure are,' Dante piped up.

'I heard you, sonny.' Barker glared at the gunman and then returned his eyes to the obvious leader of the six men. 'How long you known Mason?'

'Years, friend. Mason Dwire asked us if we could help him out,' Holt snarled.

'He did?' Barker watched as Holt nodded firmly.

'He sure did. He wants us to help him move some boxes,' Holt answered dryly as he blew smoke into the lantern-lit air. 'We owe him a favour. After we've done that, we're heading on our way.'

Barker nodded. 'That must be why Dwire rented these nags for you, I guess. He bought the buckboard a while back. Don't ask me why. That fat old bastard ain't even used it before.'

'Lawyers sure are a pretty strange breed,' Gibbs laughed as he moved up beside the rest of the gang. 'Ain't no point trying to fathom out their thinking.'

Holt inhaled smoke deep into his lungs as he watched the blacksmith with an icy stare.

'Thanks for delivering the buckboard, friend,' he said. 'We'll get it and this team of fine horses back to you as soon as it's served its purpose.'

Barker turned his powerful frame.

'Anyways, I can't stand around here chewing the fat with you all night, boys. I'll go start getting your horses saddled up. They'll be ready in about an hour.'

'I'm obliged.' Holt nodded slowly and then looked at his five followers.

The six hired gunmen watched as Barker started to amble to his aromatic livery stable. When the big man was out of earshot Gibbs moved closer to Holt.

'That critter troubles me some, Emmett,' he admitted as he rested his gloved hands on his holstered gun grips.

'He's harmless, Bart.' Holt tossed his cigar butt at the sand and then climbed up on to the driver's board. He glanced down at the five men and then pointed his thumb at the flatbed. 'Get in back, boys.'

The five gunmen moved to the rear of the buckboard and dropped its tailgate. Holt pulled out the detailed drawing the lawyer had provided for them and studied it carefully until it was branded into his mind.

'Get in back, you scum-suckers,' Holt ordered. 'We've got to get this to that warehouse and find them coffins.'

As though commanded by the Devil himself, Dante, Jones, Harper and Collins obediently climbed up on to the back of the buckboard as Gibbs hastily secured its tailgate and then ran to the front of the large vehicle. He climbed up beside Holt and picked up the heavy leathers before releasing the brake with his boot.

'Get going, Bart,' Holt snarled.

Dodge City resounded with the ear-splitting sound

of the reins being cracked above the backs of the two-horse team. The buckboard took off at breakneck speed along the main street with its cargo of deadly gunmen clinging to its boards.

At that very moment Gat Hammer emerged from the Deluxe Hotel with a toothpick in the corner of his mouth. He stopped and watched open-mouthed as the fast-moving buckboard raced past the elegant hotel.

Hammer was startled. He stepped to the edge of the boardwalk and watched them curiously as the buckboard was expertly steered into a side street.

Then a voice caught him by surprise.

'Where you headed, Gat?' it asked from behind his wide shoulders.

Hammer swung around on his high heels and stared at Tom McGee as his hand rested on the grip of his holstered six-shooter.

He sighed in relief at the familiar face and shook his head at the trail boss.

'You plumb shook me up, Tom,' he said.

'I come looking for that young kid you recommended,' McGee said as he squinted into the ornate hotel through its glass doors. 'Is he in there?'

'Nope, I ain't seen Billy for a few hours,' Hammer replied before relaxing. 'He's probably gone home to get some vittles.'

McGee rubbed his freshly shaven jaw. 'You got time for a couple of drinks, Gat?'

The Cheyenne cowboy smiled. 'Well I just finished an inch-thick steak and come to think about it, I could use a few drinks to wash it down.'

'As long as we don't run into the rest of the crew, Gat,' McGee smiled and rested a hand on the younger man's shoulder. 'I made that mistake last night. I don't hanker waking up next to Montana Mae again.'

'They say that the Long Branch is mighty slick for a saloon,' Hammer said as the two cowboys strode along the street. 'They also reckon that it's got mirrors that a party can see their faces in.'

McGee chuckled. 'Then the Long Horn it is, boy.'

'We ain't gonna get drunk are we?' Hammer wondered.

'I surely hope we find salvation before the demon drink drags us down into the bowels of hell, Gat,' the older man bellowed like a Bible-punching preacher.

Both cowboys stepped down on to the sand.

'I'll take that as a "yes" then, Tom,' Hammer grinned.

They crossed the street and aimed their boots at the well-illuminated Long Branch saloon. Yet even as they reached the saloon Hammer's mind kept thinking about the buckboard he had just witnessed racing by.

'It's doubtful we'll see any of the boys in here, Gat,' McGee said as he studied the impressive façade. 'The prices would scare even the toughest cow-puncher away.'

Hammer said nothing as his thoughts kept linger-ing on the six men in dust coats. There was something about them that kept nagging at the cowboy.

McGee placed his hand on the swing doors and was about to push them inward when he noticed the pained expression in his friend's face. Like the father figure he had become over the years, he stopped in his tracks and looked at his top wrangler.

'What's wrong, Gat?' he asked.

Hammer knew that he could not lie to McGee. The older cowboy knew him far too well. The sea-soned trail boss could read him like an open book. The Cheyenne cowboy shrugged and bit his bottom lip thoughtfully as he battled with the thoughts that dogged him.

The dust kicked up by the buckboard's wheel rims still hung in the evening air. Hammer spat the tooth-pick at the sand and shook his head.

'Damned if I know, Tom,' he admitted. 'Something's sure bothering me though. I just can't seem to figure out what it is.'

The trail boss patted the arm of his young pal.

'It'll come back to you once you've got a few drinks in you, Gat boy,' McGee smiled.

They entered the Long Branch and moved across its busy floor to the bar counter. They purchased their drinks and then sat down at one of the few vacant round tables.

No sooner had Hammer finished his first glass of beer than he knew exactly what was bothering him about the men in dust coats. His eyes widened as he sat bolt upright and snapped his fingers.

'You were right, Tom.' He smiled at McGee.

'I was?'

'You said that it'd come back to me once I had a drink. It has. Now I know what's been gnawing at my innards, Tom,' he announced as he placed the empty glass down beside the jug he and McGee were sharing beer from.

McGee raised an eyebrow. 'And what would that be exactly, Cheyenne?'

Hammer leaned across the circular table and stared his friend straight in the eyes. 'I know one of them hombres, Tom. At least I've seen him before. He was one of the outlaws I exchanged bullets with a couple of months back. He escaped but I recognize his ugly features. They're branded into my head.'

The older man rested against the back of his chair

and watched the excited young cowboy. He had known Gat Hammer since he was just a kid and knew that the youngster was rarely mistaken. If Hammer said he had seen someone before then you could bet your life on it being true.

'Are you talking about the half-dozen varmints I seen on that buckboard outside the hotel, boy?' he checked.

Hammer nodded firmly and rose to his feet.

'That's exactly who I'm talking about, Tom. Not the other critters with him but the leader of the bunch,' he stated. 'That bastard is the same critter who tried to kill me.'

The older cowboy finished his suds and pushed his hat back on to the crown of his head. He stared at the excitable Hammer; every eye within the Long Branch was also looking at the young cowboy.

'What you intending to do about it, Gat?' he asked.

Hammer thought for a moment. 'I'll go tell the marshal that there's a questionable critter in Dodge and he's got five varmints with him.'

McGee got to his feet. 'So you reckon that they're up to something, Gat? Is that why you're fit to burst?'

Hammer nodded. 'Where do you figure the marshal would be at this time of night, Tom?'

A wry smile came to the older man. He walked

around the table and headed toward the street. As he reached out to push the swing doors apart he glanced over his shoulder at his young friend.

'C'mon, Cheyenne boy,' he laughed. 'We'll find him together.'

As the cowboys left the Long Branch, its doors rocked back and forth on their hinges. Mason Dwire had listened to every word that had spilled from the young cowboy's mouth and knew that it meant trouble for him and the men he had just sent out to undertake the most daring robbery in Dodge City's short history. Dwire had been seated between Foster and Chester and the bottle of whiskey they had been savouring. The devious banker rose to his feet and patted them both on their shoulders. His watery eyes glanced at the wall clock just above a ten-foot long mirror before checking his own pocket watch. They tallied.

'Thanks for the drinks, gentlemen. I'll see you later,' the lawyer said. 'I've got something to do.'

The lawyer checked his cuffs and then walked out into the cool night air. The imported Scottish whisky had not taken its toll on the lawyer as it had on both Foster and Chester. Spurred on by his encouragement, the still-seated pair were well on the way toward being drunk. The lawyer considered that a bonus to be added to his carefully thought-out scheme.

Mason Dwire paused on the boardwalk as the cool air brushed his thoughtful face. His eyes tightened and watched the two cowboys heading through the lantern light in the direction of the marshal's office.

The last thing Holt and his gang needed was interrupting, Dwire thought. Once they had emptied the safe in the Cattleman Club and delivered its precious cargo to the train, he did not care what happened to any of them. But they had to be able to fulfil his detailed scheme.

The rotund figure moved to a brightly painted porch upright and rested a shoulder against it. Dwire was not a man who ever got involved in any of the outrageous plans his crooked mind created but a sense of panic was brewing within him. His heart pounded inside his expensive attire.

'That young cowpuncher is going to ruin everything,' he mumbled under his breath as he pulled a twin-barrelled derringer from his vest pocket and cocked its hammers. 'I can't allow him to mess this up by getting the marshal chasing Holt and his boys. It'll ruin everything. No righteous cowpoke is going to spoil this for me. I have to stop him.'

He gripped the small weapon in his hand and began following both Hammer and McGee into the darker part of Dodge City. It had not occurred to the lawyer previously but the further a soul ventured

111

from the large saloon, the darker it became.

He was grateful that the cowboys were talking and not striding as quickly as he knew they were capable of. His short legs ached as he kept pace with them. The gun in his hand was barely visible as Dwire slipped between the shadows in pursuit.

It was completely out of character for the lawyer ever to deviate from his well-considered plans but his guts told him that he had to silence them before they were able to tell Marshal Grey about Holt and his cohorts.

The lawyer had killed his fair share of men in his time but that had been long ago when he had been able to see his feet and had the agility of youth.

Beads of sweat trailed down his face in defiance of the cool night air. The bulky character carefully gained on the cowboys. They had to die, and die before either of them could talk to the marshal, his mind screamed at him.

There were few street lanterns perched on top of poles in this part of Dodge. What light there was came from the store fronts which were still open for business. The further the cowboys walked to the marshal's office, the darker it became.

Had Dwire realized that the younger cowboy he was trailing was the same hombre that he had read the exaggerated tales about in the newspaper months before, the lawyer might have been more cautious. But in Dodge City every cowboy looked alike to men like Dwire. The only difference was how drunk they were after selling their herd.

A fury was fermenting like a volcano inside the rotund lawyer as his watery eyes stared at the backs of both men ahead of him. Backs which he intended putting bullets into when he was close enough. His hand was sweating as it gripped the small derringer. His finger curled around the weapon's triggers and stroked them.

His volcano was about to erupt. He raised his arm and levelled the gun as both cowboys turned a corner and entered a dark side street.

Mason Dwire defied his own physique and ran the thirty-foot distance to the corner. He was panting like an old hound dog as he rested his shoulder on the wooden edge of the wall and looked at the two barely visible cowboys as they headed to where lantern light spilled from the marshal's office on to the sand. The lawyer closed one eye, raised the derringer and held it at arm's length.

He aimed.

ELEVEN

Unaware that they were being targeted, Hammer and McGee made their way deeper into the dimly lit side street. The only illumination came from the marshal's small office. A wall lantern competed with the lamplight which cascaded from the windows of the structure.

'Reckon the marshal's in there, Gat boy?' McGee wondered as they closed the distance between themselves and the eerie light.

'I sure hope so,' Hammer sighed. 'I don't wanna try and find him in a town as big as Dodge. It'll take forever.'

The older cowboy looked around the narrow street. He was not impressed by what he saw. This was probably the oldest and most rundown part of the cattle town and it was showing its age.

'I got me a feeling they don't respect the law around these parts.' McGee gestured at their surroundings. 'This is the most sorrowful damn street I ever done seen and I've done seen a lot of sorrowful looking streets.'

Suddenly without warning the narrow confines of the street lit up as two white flashes carved a route through the darkness from the corner to the main street. The noise was deafening as the two shots tore into the cowboys. McGee buckled as he felt the impact of the derringer bullet hit him in his broad back. Hammer staggered as the second deadly bullet knocked him forward. A fiery pain ripped through him as though he had been struck by a lightning bolt. With blood trailing from his temple the dazed cowboy dragged his six-shooter from its holster and twisted around.

McGee fell on to his face beside his stunned pal's boots.

Hammer raised his weapon and blasted two shots in reply before he steadied himself beside McGee. The eyes of the famed Cheyenne cowboy darted to his comrade and then back at the corner.

'Don't worry, Tom.' Hammer spat at the sand and moved toward their hidden attacker. 'I'll make that hombre pay for shooting at us.'

Hammer blasted another two shots into the darkness.

As chunks of wood were ripped from the corner he was resting behind, Dwire poked two fresh bullets into the smoking chambers of his derringer. He drew the weapon's hammers back and then looked around the corner at the defiant cowboy who vainly tried to find a target to shoot at. Unlike Hammer, Mason Dwire could see his chosen prey clearly.

'Eat lead, cowpoke,' the lawyer mumbled and squeezed both triggers at the same moment. The derringer bullets hit the gun in Hammer's out-held hand. An octopus of blinding sparks erupted from the gun in the cowboy's grasp. No mule could have kicked harder. The dazzling light caused the cowboy to fall back. He fell heavily beside his already prostrate companion and felt the back of his skull impact on the ground.

Darkness suddenly engulfed Hammer. He felt himself sinking into the bottomless pit of unconsciousness. The cowboy vainly tried to claw himself back but nothing could save him from the inevitable. It was as though quicksand was swallowing him and he could do nothing to prevent it.

The shadowy corner of the narrow side street saw the balding head of the lawyer as he looked upon his handiwork with the smoking derringer in his hand.

116

A sickening smile etched his sweating features as his watery eyes stared at the two cowboys lying in the lamp light of the marshal's office. Neither cowboy moved. Dwire gave a satisfied grunt.

He had done what he had come to do.

'Problem solved.' Dwire smugly turned and hurried along the main street away from his deadly handiwork. He moved quickly for a big man and within a few beats of his racing heart had vanished into the multitude of people in search of their own place to find satisfaction.

Nobody noticed the fat old lawyer as he melted into the crowd. Nobody apart from the buxom Montana Mae as she leaned against the porch upright outside her place of business. The female tilted her well-powdered face as she recognized the stout lawyer hurrying back into the better part of town. Dwire was one of her most regular of clients and perhaps the most talkative.

Mae watched him weave his way between the other men and women who filled the boardwalk along the main street. She knew that the pompous lawyer was up to something for he had blurted it out during one of their many meetings.

Dwire talked in his sleep.

Two and two often make four. Mae had heard the gunshots but unlike everyone else in the lantern-lit street, she knew they were not simply from men letting off steam. Her eyes focused on the smoke that trailed the lawyer, filtering through his fingers as he clutched the still-smouldering weapon.

That intrigued the fallen angel.

She had been wondering when he might start to put his dreams into cold-blooded action.

Her well-plucked eyebrows rose.

'Now where would old Dwire be going in such a hurry?' she asked herself before placing a cigarette into the corner of her mouth and igniting a match with her long painted fingernails. 'Maybe I oughta find out.'

Mae tossed the match over her naked shoulder and started to follow the wealthy lawyer. She was not going to let the chance of making a few extra bucks slip through her supple fingers.

The mature lady of the night crossed the street in pursuit of her panting prey. She sucked hard on the cigarette in a fashion that was well practised. Then a tall, handsome gambler known as Lucky O'Hara stepped out from the brightly illuminated Deluxe Hotel and tipped his white Stetson at Montana Mae.

'Ma'am,' he said respectfully. His grin and flashing eyes stopped the female in her tracks. She pulled the cigarette from her red lips and fluttered her eyelashes at the gambler.

'Well howdy, stranger,' she purred and stepped closer to O'Hara. 'I ain't seen you before.'

Lucky O'Hara checked the wad of notes he had just won in a private game of stud poker and then slid them between the leather leaves of his wallet.

'You ain't bin looking in the right places, ma'am,' he said before returning his wallet to his inside jacket pocket.

She moved closer to him. So close he could not fail to stare down into her cavernous cleavage. 'Are you lonesome, stranger?'

'Not now, dear lady,' O'Hara sighed as her perfume filled his flared nostrils and glanced around the crowded street. 'I'd ask you if you might care to spend the rest of this fine night in my company but it looks as though you're in a hurry.'

Mae dismissed all thoughts of continuing after the lawyer as she pressed her satin covered thigh against the gambler's tailored pants. Her eyes sparkled in the amber light.

'I'm in no hurry, handsome,' she said as her long fingernails stroked his coat lapel. 'I've got all the time in the world to keep you company and I know that you've got the money.'

'I don't normally do this sort of thing, ma'am,' O'Hara lied.

'Neither do I,' Mae grinned. 'This is my night to

119

go Bible reading but too much reading can put a strain on a gal's eyes.'

Lucky O'Hara held out his arm. Montana Mae slid her naked arm around his elbow and they both started to stroll back toward her place of business.

Back in the dark, narrow side street the door of the marshal's office swung open. Light washed across the two men sprawled upon the sand. A pool of blood had united the cowboys as it spread from their wounds.

Marshal Cole Grey was first to emerge from the confines of the small structure. He held a scattergun across his middle as he glanced around the dark buildings that flanked them. He then stared at the two motionless cowboys on the sand.

'Get out here, Ben,' he ordered from the corner of his mouth to his eager deputy. 'Check them cow-punchers.'

The deputy moved around the shoulders of his superior with a .45 in his right hand. He cautiously moved through the amber light to where both McGee and Hammer lay.

Grey stepped to the edge of the boardwalk and curled his finger around the triggers of his massive shotgun. His eyes continued to dart from one shadow to the next in search of the unknown gunman who had left the bleeding cowboys like discarded trash outside his small office.

Graff knelt between Hammer and McGee. His head swung until he was looking at the burly marshal.

'We met these critters before, Marshal,' he announced before returning his eyes to the bleeding men. 'This is the trail boss and this is the critter the newspapers call the Cheyenne cowboy.'

Marshal Grey stepped down from the boardwalk and approached his deputy. His eyes still searched the shadows that surrounded them.

'Are you sure?' Grey asked without looking down at the men before him.

'Yep. I'm gonna get some water,' Graff nodded, got to his feet and rushed to the office. He returned within seconds with a canteen and dropped on to his knees between the men.

'Are they dead?' Grey asked dryly.

'I ain't sure, Marshal,' the deputy answered as he raised the head of the younger man and carefully poured water into his mouth. The words had only just left Graff's lips when Hammer spluttered and coughed as he regained consciousness.

Marshal Grey watched as his deputy then moved to the body of the older cowboy. The marshal moved around the cowboys at his feet with his long double-barrelled weapon aimed at the darkness.

Graff looked up at his boss. 'This one ain't bin so

lucky, Marshal. He's got a bullet in the middle of his back. I reckon it went straight through his heart.'

Cole Grey looked down at the lifeless form of Tom McGee and the bullet hole in his wide back. The lamplight from his office illuminated the pool of blood which covered the leather vest of the trail boss.

'Damn it all,' the marshal cursed. 'Who'd wanna kill old Tom McGee? It don't make any sense.'

The deputy used the canteen water to wash the blood from the gash on Hammer's forehead. The cowboy was groggy and as helpless as a kitten.

'What's going on?' Hammer muttered.

'You'll be OK, Cheyenne,' Graff said as he pushed the stopper back into the neck of the canteen.

'Help Cheyenne up and take him to the office, Ben,' Grey mumbled at his deputy as he crouched and pushed his fingertips into the neck of McGee in search of a pulse. He gritted his teeth and then stood back up as his deputy's assumption was confirmed. 'He's dead OK.'

Both lawmen assisted the dazed cowboy into the bright office and helped him to a hard-back chair. Hammer sat and stared blankly at his surroundings as his head slowly cleared.

Graff looked at the gash across the cowboy's temple.

'Hell, you sure are lucky, Cheyenne,' he stated as

he checked the graze and dabbed more water over the unsightly wound. 'You could have had your head split wide open if that bullet had bin an inch to the left.'

The cold water awoke the cowboy from the delirium which had smothered his thoughts. He suddenly began to recall why he and his pal had been heading to the marshal's office.

'I came to tell you that there are six varmints in Dodge, Marshal,' he sighed heavily as Grey placed his scattergun on to his untidy desk. 'One of them is the dude I had my ruckus with a few months back.'

'I read about that, Cheyenne,' Graff nodded.

'Who is he?' Grey asked the cowboy.

Hammer shook his head. 'Damned if I know but I killed some of his gang back then. He's rustled himself up a new bunch and they're here, Marshal. I got me a gut feeling that they're planning something big.'

The deputy looked excited. 'You figure they're here to rob the bank or something, Cheyenne?'

'Damned if I know,' Hammer answered as he nursed his throbbing head. 'All I can tell you is that the hombre has five fresh gun-toting followers with him. A man like that don't herd a bunch of gunmen together coz he's lonesome.'

Graff looked to the marshal. 'Cheyenne's right.'

123

Marshal Grey shook his head and moved to his coffee pot on the top of his pot-belly stove. He filled a tin cup and blew at the steam.

'I ain't seen any strangers in town, Cheyenne,' he said dismissively.

'Me neither,' the deputy agreed. 'But Dodge is a mighty big place. A man could hide a small army in town if he's a mind to do so.'

Grey shrugged. 'I guess so but I still ain't seen any strangers.'

Hammer nursed his pounding skull in the palms of his hands as he tried to gather his thoughts. He then looked up at both the lawmen.

'Where's Tom?' he asked.

Grey and Graff glanced at one another and then the marshal placed a hand on the shoulder of the seated cowboy. He inhaled deeply.

'Tom's dead, Cheyenne,' he informed him.

Hammer could not believe the words that he had just heard. He got back to his feet and brushed both star packers aside as he walked to the open doorway.

He stared open-mouthed at the horrific sight on the sand outside the office. The lifeless body of McGee lay upon the lamplit sand. The blood which covered his friend's body sparkled like rubies.

The cowboy turned his head and looked at both lawmen.

'He's dead?' he stammered.

Grey nodded and sipped his black beverage. 'I'm afraid so, Cheyenne. I reckon he must have bin dead before he hit the ground, boy. Go get the doc, Ben,' the marshal ordered. 'Cheyenne's hurt as well.'

'I don't need no sawbones, Marshal,' Hammer said quietly as he returned to the chair and sat down.

'I'm real sorry, Cheyenne,' Marshal Grey said as he rested a hip on the desk and stared through the steam of his coffee at the youngster. 'I know you and Tom have bin pals for a real long time.'

Hammer looked up at the lawman. 'Don't that prove that my suspicions are right, Marshal? We were coming here to tell you about that galoot I tangled with a few months back and suddenly somebody uses us for target practice.'

'It could be a coincidence, Cheyenne,' Grey sighed. 'Dodge is full of back-shooters at the best of times.'

'No, it weren't no back-shooter.' Hammer shook his head. 'I figure that someone tried to silence us before we had a chance to tell you about that varmint, Marshal.'

'It's a pity you don't know his name,' the marshal sighed. 'If we had a name there might be a chance of his image being on one of my circulars.'

Graff looked at the cowboy. 'You might not know

his name but I bet he knows yours, Cheyenne.'

The cowboy looked at the deputy.

'How'd you figure that?' Hammer pressed a thumb knuckle into his pounding brow.

'Everyone who read about that incident knows your name, Cheyenne,' the deputy added. 'You're the Cheyenne cowboy. Hell, you're famous.'

Hammer stared at Grey. 'The deputy could be right. It seems that ever since we brought that herd to the railhead every man, woman and child has bin calling me Cheyenne.'

'Just like the newspaper story,' Graff nodded. 'I bet he knows that you're here in Dodge and that's why you were shot at. I reckon you're right, Cheyenne. It all figures.'

Marshal Grey took another sip of his strong coffee. 'It could still be just a coincidence.'

'I don't believe in coincidences, Marshal,' Hammer said through gritted teeth. 'We were deliberately shot at to try and stop us alerting you. Something big is gonna happen in Dodge. Mark my words.'

Grey was just about reply when the sound of a horse being ridden hard echoed around the building. All three men looked at the open doorway as a rider dragged rein outside the open doorway and dismounted.

'That's one of the telegraph linesmen, Marshal,' the deputy said as the rider dropped from his mount and hurried into the office.

The dust-caked linesman was exhausted. He staggered into the office and tried to catch his breath. The marshal lowered his cup from his lips.

'What's wrong, boy?' Grey asked the excited rider.

'We got mighty big trouble, Marshal,' the linesman panted and pointed at the dark street.

Grey frowned as he studied the figure.

'What kinda trouble?' he asked.

The man moved closer to all three of his observers. 'I was sent by the telegraph operator to check the wires. He wanted me to find out why his keys went dead earlier. I found out why OK. Some galoot has shot down every damn wire in the canyon and it's gonna take a couple of days to fix. But that ain't the worst of it.'

'It ain't?' The marshal stared at the lineman.

'Nope, it sure ain't,' the trembling linesman nodded frantically. 'Whoever cut the wires also killed the telegraph operator at the water station. Shot the poor critter dead in his office, Marshal.'

The deputy moved closer to the marshal; Grey stared into his black beverage as the realization of what was happening suddenly began to dawn on him.

'Another killing?' Grey said in disbelief.

'With the telegraph wires down we can't send or receive any messages, Marshal,' Graff said nervously. 'Dodge City is all on its lonesome. We're on our lonesome.'

Hammer looked at the marshal.

'He's right. Now do you think I'm fretting over nothing? Now do you understand why I think that galoot I tussled with a few months ago is here in Dodge to do something real bad, Marshal?'

Marshal Grey stared at Hammer and began to nod at the cowboy. 'You might be right, Cheyenne. Maybe there ain't no such things as coincidences after all.'

'What we gonna do, Marshal?' the deputy asked.

'First you're gonna go to the funeral parlour and tell him to come and get Tom's body off the sand,' Grey said before pointing at the linesman. 'And you rustle up a team of boys and try and get them wires fixed as fast as you can.'

'What about the old man up in the station box?' the linesman asked.

Grey looked at the telegraph worker. 'Don't go fretting, son. I'll tell the undertaker to head on up there when he comes to collect Tom.'

Hammer scratched his jaw.

'What are we gonna do, Marshal?' he wondered.

'We're gonna start hunting the bastards who've

bin killing folks around here, Cheyenne,' the weath-ered lawman replied as he donned his hat, grabbed his scattergun and headed for the street. 'I don't like folks getting gunned down in my town. It kinda riles me.'

Hammer quickly reloaded his .45 and then slid it into his holster. He watched as the marshal paused on the boardwalk outside his office and stared at the lifeless body of Tom McGee. He curled his finger at Hammer.

'C'mon,' he said.

TWELVE

Walt Kitter had done many jobs over the years before being given the job of caretaker to the Cattleman Club. The job had proven to be easy money until this eventful night. Death had come swiftly and caught the old timer by surprise when he had made the mistake of confronting Emmett Holt.

The bearded old man was seated against a wall in a pool of his own blood with a stiletto in his chest just behind the double doors of the side entrance of the club. Holt ushered Jones and Collins out into the dark alley for the final time with the metal coffin between them. As they loaded the third and last coffin on to the flatbed buckboard with the assistance of the others, Holt walked back into the club and stared down at his handiwork. Kitter still wore the same shocked expression on his face, but now it was nothing more than a death mask.

The aged caretaker had not stood a chance against the thin-bladed dagger that Holt had thrust into his bony chest. The stiletto's long blade had punctured the old timer's heart before emerging out of his back.

Emmett Holt seldom used the knife but when he did it was with force and expert accuracy. Few men who had stood toe-to-toe with the infamous gunman had lived to tell the tale. He leaned down and gripped the silver handle of the weapon and pulled it from the caretaker's chest with ease. Holt glared at the lifeless eyes of the old man and chuckled to himself as he wiped the gore from its razor-sharp blade on Kitter's shirt.

'We've loaded the last one of them coffins, Emmett,' Gibbs said from behind Holt's wide shoulders as he slid the dagger back into its hiding place.

'I'm finished here too, Bart,' Holt said. 'I just had to extract my pig sticker.'

Gibbs glanced down at the body propped against the interior wall of the club. 'Is he dead, Emmett?'

'He's dead OK,' Holt replied.

Holt swung on his heels and walked out into the alley. He closed the doors behind them and watched as Dante secured the buckboard's tailgate with metal pins. He waved his hands at the lethal bunch.

131

'Get on board, boys,' he hissed like a devilish sidewinder as he pushed his dust coat tails over his holstered gun grips and walked along the heavily laden vehicle. 'We're gonna take it nice and easy. We don't wanna draw any attention to ourselves until we've loaded these three coffins on the train.'

The five men clambered on to the buckboard as Holt climbed up on to its driver's board beside Gibbs. His deadly eyes flashed in the eerie light as Gibbs.

'Nice and easy, Bart,' he growled as he bit the end off a cigar and spat it from their high perch. 'Take it nice and easy.'

Gibbs nodded back at Holt, released the brake pole and then cracked the reins across the backs of both horses. The large vehicle began to move slowly through the shadows on its way to the awaiting loco-motive.

The lantern-lit streets of Dodge continued to defy the night and were steadily getting busier as the town's clocks slowly headed toward midnight. The scent of stale perfume hung along its boardwalks as the ladies of the night started to appear in nearly every vacant doorway. Yet no matter how crowded the gambling halls, brothels and saloons became it meant nothing to the odd pair of tall men as they strolled into the very heart of the famed cattle town.

Both the cowboy and the marshal had only one thing on their minds. The mutual thought that somewhere in Dodge there were six heavily armed men, who they suspected were responsible for the growing death toll, gnawed at their craws.

Gat Hammer walked shoulder-to-shoulder beside the troubled Cole Grey in search of their elusive prey. There was a slim chance that the half-dozen men in their long dust coats had nothing to do with the brutal murders, but neither the cowboy nor the lawman believed in coincidences.

Grey looked at Hammer and then pointed across the wide street to the bank. As they strode toward the building they could see the construction workers busily adding a stone outer layer to its wooden fabric.

Grey paused and rubbed his thick neck muscles.

'Don't reckon this is their target, Cheyenne,' the lawman said drily as his eyes surveyed the brightly illuminated structure. 'They'd have to be loco if they tried to rob this bank with all these stonemasons around.'

The Cheyenne cowboy agreed with his newly found friend as he rested a boot on the boardwalk and watched as the highly skilled masons went about their duties reinforcing the bank.

'You're right, Marshal,' he said. 'This ain't it.

There must be someplace else around here that has enough money to have tempted them hombres into Dodge.'

'Yeah, but what?' Grey spat at the sand and turned to stare at the line of buildings opposite them. The Cattleman Club was closed and shuttered for the night. His eyes passed its dim façade without giving it a second thought. 'There's another bank around the corner. Maybe that's their target.'

Hammer nodded and moved to the side of the lawman.

'Let's go check it out, Marshal,' he said as he rested his hand on his gun grip.

They headed slowly toward the corner. Both men barely uttered a word to one another as they rounded the corner and started to pace toward the far smaller bank. The red brick structure had two bright coal-tar lanterns directly outside its metal-framed door. Grey tested the door and then looked back at his companion.

'This one seems secure enough,' the marshal muttered as he walked back to the cowboy. The bank's lanterns spilled glowing light all across the street as Grey stepped up to the young cowboy. He stared long and hard at Hammer and then grabbed his chin, turning his head to the left. The gash was bleeding again. Blood was flowing freely down the cowboy's chiselled features.

'That graze sure looks bad, boy,' Grey stated bluntly. 'It needs stitching up.'

Hammer rubbed the back of his hand across the side of his face. He was surprised by the amount of crimson gore upon his knuckles.

'We ain't got time to get me stitched up, Marshal,' he said before glancing around the street. He had never noticed how many females there were in Dodge, but he had never been there sober before. 'Let's keep looking for the bastard who tried his utmost to kill me a while back.'

Grey removed his bandanna and handed it to the cowboy. 'Wrap this wipe around your head, Cheyenne. It'll mop up most of the blood until we can get that wound tended.'

Hammer did as the older man suggested and tied a firm knot in the cotton bandanna. 'I bet I look like a real dumb ass wearing this.'

Grey grinned. 'You looked like a real dumb ass before you tied my wipe around your head, boy.'

Both men began to continue their search when three or four of Hammer's cowboy pals were thrown from a gambling hall and landed in the dusty street just ahead of them.

'You know them dirt-suckers, Cheyenne?' Grey asked as he cradled the scattergun across his belly.

Hammer nodded. 'Yep, they're trail pals of mine.'

Grey watched as the three men scrambled to their feet and went to charge back into the gambling hall. Hammer raised his hand and stopped them.

'Hold on there, boys,' the cowboy shouted at the trio of blood-splattered wranglers. 'I got something to tell you.'

One by one their eyes fixed upon Hammer. One by one they smiled at their friend.

'Where you bin, boy?' Chuck Vale wondered as he steadied himself in the middle of the small group.

'What's so plumb important you stand between your amigos and a good fight, Cheyenne?' Cookie Bray smiled as he checked his teeth.

'What's so damn serious, Cheyenne?' Larry Pike chortled as he rested against a hitching rail. 'How come you're wearing that neckerchief on your damn head?'

The face of Hammer was grim as he lowered his head and told them about Tom McGee's killing. For a moment none of the four cowboys said anything as they seemed to instantly sober up.

'Tom's dead?' Cookie said sadly.

Hammer nodded. 'Yep, he's dead OK and I'm bleeding up a storm.'

'Who killed him, Cheyenne?' Pike asked.

'That's what me and the marshal are trying to find

out,' Hammer sighed as he noticed the lawman stare over at the swing doors of a saloon a few yards away from the gambling establishment.

Marshal Grey looked to Hammer and shook his head.

'They ain't in there either,' Grey said.

Cookie marched up to the marshal and stared straight into his seasoned face. 'We'll help you look for the hombre that killed Tom, Marshal.'

Grey suddenly noticed that Hammer's colleagues no longer looked like drunken fools. They suddenly appeared to be sober and serious.

Deadly serious.

Suddenly their attention was drawn to the rattling of the well-laden buckboard as it emerged from a back street and was turned toward the railhead. Hammer stepped away from his four companions and squinted through the strange amber light at the vehicle that approached them.

'What's wrong, Cheyenne?' the marshal asked.

For a moment the cowboy did not reply. His entire concentration was fixed upon the figures he could barely make out aboard the buckboard. Hammer was about to turn away when his eyes narrowed upon the familiar figure sat beside the driver.

The hair on Hammer's neck began to rise. 'Take a long hard look at that critter, boys.'

The three other cowboys stepped forward and flanked Hammer as they peered through the gloom at the figures who were driving through the amber light.

It was Chuck Vale who spoke first. 'That sure looks like the varmint that you locked horns with a while back, Cheyenne.'

Hammer nodded. 'That's what I was thinking.'

'Is that the hombres we've bin looking for, Cheyenne boy?' Grey asked his youthful friend. 'Well? Is it?'

'It sure is, Marshal,' Hammer nodded, stepping off the boardwalk and walking to the middle of the sandy street. The buckboard continued on toward the men who were watching its steady approach. The marshal and the three cowboys strode into the centre of the street and stood just behind Hammer.

Grey swung his scattergun up and levelled it at the men sat high on the driver's board. He cocked its hammers and moved to the side of Hammer before aiming at the heavens.

'Hold on up there,' Marshal Grey ordered, waving his long barrelled scattergun like a warning flag. 'I want some words with you.'

'Keep driving, Bart,' Holt growled as he pulled one of his .45s from its holster. 'Don't stop for that fat old star packer.'

138

Reluctantly, Gibbs obeyed and slapped the reins hard across the backs of the two sturdy horses. The buckboard gathered speed.

The street rocked as the marshal squeezed on one of his mighty weapon's triggers. A plume of blinding light exploded from one of the shotgun's barrels as it sent buckshot into the stars.

'Stop,' Grey loudly repeated.

To his utter surprise the vehicle did not stop or even slow. It just charged straight at them as its passengers pulled their six-shooters free.

As the cowboys and the startled lawman looked on, the six-shooters unleashed their venomous fury at them. Bullets passed within inches of the cowboys as the marshal dragged his Peacemaker free of its holster.

More shots rang out. Their red-hot tapers cut through the shadows causing all five men to duck and dive for cover.

As bullets peppered the sand around his boots, Hammer pushed the lawman to the side a fraction of a heartbeat before the buckboard hurtled between them. The wide-eyed team of sturdy horses charged, Hammer threw his long body to the side. He drew his .45 and blasted a shot up at the men on the buckboard. As his bullet embedded itself into the side lumber of the fast-moving vehicle he felt his left leg being hit by one of the horses. Hammer span like a child's spinning top in the air before hitting the sand. He rolled over and over before coming to a violent stop beside a water trough.

Hammer cocked his gun hammer again and blasted another wild shot in reply. Then he saw the hauntingly familiar face of Holt as it stared through the gunsmoke and fired down at him.

Hammer rolled back.

A bullet went clean through the trough sending a torrent of water to flow between himself and Holt.

The air filled with the deafening overture of guns being fired from not only Holt but his men on the flatbed. The sand kicked up all around the men on the ground as the fast-moving vehicle skidded around a corner and vanished from sight.

With the sound of gunfire still ringing in his ears, Hammer forced his long frame off the ground and winced as he put his weight on his leg. He gritted his teeth as the dust finally began to settle.

'You hurt, Cheyenne?' Grey's distinctive voice bellowed out from across the street.

As the dust thinned, Hammer caught sight of the marshal as he clambered back to his feet. 'I'm OK. One of them horses caught my shin.'

'Is it broke?' Grey called out as he steadied himself against a hitching pole.

Hammer started to limp toward the marshal. 'It ain't busted.'

As the Cheyenne cowboy neared the lawman his eyes caught sight of his three pals. They were lying where the horses had thrown them. Hammer moved as quickly as he could to the cowboys.

'Chuck? Cookie? Larry? Are you boys OK?' he questioned their motionless bodies. 'Quit play-acting.'

Marshal Grey had been winded by being pushed out of the path of the charging horses but refused to let the younger man see his discomfort. He walked past Hammer to the cowboys and knelt between them. He turned and glanced at Hammer.

'They ain't dead,' he sighed. 'They're just knocked out.'

Hammer felt a sense of relief flow over him as the marshal walked to a trough, removed his hat and filled its bowl with water.

'This'll wake them up,' Grey grunted before emptying the water over Vale to awaken the cowboy. He repeated the action two more times and then stared at the dazed cowboys as they slowly clambered back to their feet.

Hammer rubbed his leg and stomped it on the ground a few times as he tried to bring it back to life.

'Them pals of yours got their noses bloodied but

they're in better shape than old Tom,' Grey muttered to Hammer. 'You sure that leg of yours is OK, Cheyenne?'

'It's sore but it's OK, Marshal,' Hammer said as he straightened up and stared through the dust. 'Where do you reckon that heard of varmints were headed?'

Grey rested a hand on Hammer's shoulder. 'The only thing down in that direction is the railroad, boy.'

'Why'd you reckon they didn't stop when you told them to, Marshal?' the cowboy wondered. 'That seems mighty strange to me. It just don't figure.'

The sound of pounding hoofs rang out behind them. Both Grey and Hammer turned and stared at the solitary horseman who was cantering toward them.

Deputy Ben Graff pulled back on his long leathers and halted the mare. He leaned down from the saddle to Grey and whispered in the marshal's ear.

Grey's face went ashen.

'What's wrong, Marshal?' Hammer asked the lawman.

'There's bin another killing, Cheyenne,' Grey muttered in disbelief. 'Somebody just stabbed the old Cattleman Club caretaker. His body was discovered by the club chairman a few minutes ago.'

Hammer's eyes narrowed. 'The Cattleman Club is

where the cattle agents hold their money.'

'The money's all gone, Cheyenne,' Graff said as he steadied his mount. 'Mr Chester said the safe was cleaned out. Every last cent was stolen.'

Grey rubbed his jaw.

'They must have taken the bank's money as well,' he reasoned. 'The bank has bin putting its money in the club safe since they started reinforcing the building.'

In sudden realization, Hammer grabbed his shirt pocket and felt his bank book. His face went pale as his cowboy pals gathered around him and the pair of lawmen.

'They must have gotten your money as well, Cheyenne,' Larry Pike noted. 'That's where you've bin saving your money, ain't it?'

'Yep, it is,' Hammer said dryly before glaring along the street. 'So that's why they didn't stop. They must have had the money on that flatbed.'

Grey patted the cowboy. 'I bet you're right about them having the Cattleman money on that wagon, boy.'

Hammer looked into Grey's eyes and shook his head. It had suddenly dawned on him that his entire life savings were part of the stolen money.

'Not the Cattleman's money. They got my money, Marshal.' He growled like a tiger. 'Them bastards got my money.'

The cowboy limped to the deputy, hauled him off the horse and then swung himself up and on to its saddle. He steadied the mare and looked at them in turn.

'Get yourselves some horses and follow me,' Hammer said as he gathered up the reins. 'I gotta catch them hombres and get my money back.'

Marshal Grey vainly attempted to halt the angry cowboy but Hammer was far too skilled a horseman to be so easily stopped. He expertly backed the horse away from the lawman and then whipped the horse's shoulders. Hammer spurred hard. They watched him race off in the same direction that the buckboard had taken.

'Where in tarnation is Cheyenne going, Marshal?' Graff asked.

Ignoring the question, the marshal pointed at the saddle horses tethered to hitching poles along the street and feverishly gestured to the cowboys to round them up.

'Get some damn horseflesh for us, boys. We got us some thieving killers to catch and kill,' Grey grunted.

The deputy watched as the experienced cowboys obeyed the marshal's orders and then looked at his superior. 'Ain't stealing horses a hanging offence, Marshal?'

The older lawman rolled his eyes and then

slapped the deputy behind his left ear.

'We ain't stealing these nags, boy,' Grey explained as Vale, Bray and Pike brought five horses to the lawmen. 'We're just borrowing them.'

The five men mounted, slapped leather and then thundered through the hoof dust in pursuit of the Cheyenne cowboy.

THIRTEEN

Mason Dwire had only just arrived at the private railroad car when he heard the sound of gunshots ringing out in the heart of Dodge. His heart pounded as he scrambled from the rented buggy and watched the small one-horse vehicle hastily driven away from the length of the long carriages. He mopped the sweat from his face and squinted through the dimly lit stockyards. The sound of the gunshots still echoed around the vast yards and chilled the lawyer to the bone.

'Something's gone wrong,' he mumbled to himself as he nervously looked around the enormous yard. 'Holt and his boys must have hit trouble. Mighty big trouble by the sound of it.'

Defying the night chill, sweat literally poured from his balding scalp and flowed over his plump features.

146

This was not part of his well-constructed scheme. Now everything was in jeopardy and he knew it. Even getting out of Dodge City with the stolen money would prove no easy task.

Dwire was already physically exhausted and yet he knew that the night was far from over. His shaking fingers located the derringer in his vest pocket. He used the light which spilled out from the private car's length of windows to remove the two spent casings from the twin-barrelled gun and then he nervously reloaded. The derringer might be small but Dwire knew it was capable of killing. He had proven that when he had gunned down the two cowboys.

The troubled lawyer could hear the rattling chains of the buckboard's team as they carved a trail through the sprawling streets of Dodge. With each beat of his labouring heart Dwire could tell the buckboard was getting ever closer.

Then his watery eyes spotted the cloud of dust as the buckboard hurtled through the unmarked entrance of the stockyards. The metal wheel rims skidded on the moonlit ground as it continued to charge toward the stationary locomotive. Dwire nervously watched as the driver whipped the team mercilessly and closed in on the train.

Gibbs pushed his boot down hard on the brake pole and pulled the long leathers up to his chest.

147

The buckboard abruptly stopped beside the passenger car.

The lawyer had never seen Holt quite as flustered as he appeared to be as he and the rest of the hired gunmen dropped down from the buckboard.

'Get that damn baggage car opened up,' Holt commanded as he stood beside the train and extracted the spent cartridges from his smoking gun chambers. 'Hurry up.'

Dwire stepped toward the devilish gunfighter. 'Was that you boys doing all the shooting a few minutes back, Emmett?'

Holt glanced from his six-shooter to the lawyer.

'Sure it was us. We run into a spot of trouble as we were driving through town on our way here,' Holt replied before snapping the chamber back into the body of the gun. 'Why?'

The lawyer rubbed his many chins. 'It's just that you look kinda troubled, that's all.'

Gibbs slid the door of the baggage car open. 'I got it open, Emmett.'

'Right.' The leader of the group snapped his fingers at the others. 'The rest of you boys get them coffins loaded in there as fast as you can.'

Holt turned and scratched a match along the side of the buckboard as his men began to unload their valuable cargo and carry the hefty coffins toward the baggage car.

'You look spooked, Emmett,' the lawyer noted as Holt inhaled the toxic smoke of his last cigar. 'I ain't never seen you look like this. Anybody would think that you just seen a ghost.'

Holt exhaled and glanced into the large watery eyes of the fat lawyer. He gave a sudden nod of his head.

'Maybe I did see a ghost, Mason,' he drawled as his teeth gripped the cigar. 'We were riding down the main street on our way here. We were driving nice and slow just like you told us in your notes when the street was blocked.'

'That don't sound like any ghosts I've heard tell of.' Dwire smiled as he watched the gunmen labouring under the weight of the coffin they were attempting to slide into the baggage car.

Holt leaned over the rotund lawyer and stared straight into Dwire's soul. 'It was the marshal and a bunch of critters blocking the street, Mason. Then right in the middle of them stood the Cheyenne cowboy.'

Mason Dwire suddenly stopped grinning. He felt his heartbeat stagger inside his sweat-soaked shirt.

'That ain't possible, Emmett,' he stammered. 'I shot and killed the Cheyenne cowboy as he was headed for the marshal's office. Him and an older

149

cowpoke was going there. I killed them both before they had a chance of spilling the beans.'

Holt raised an eyebrow.

'What you talking about, Mason?' he growled. 'Me and the boys just seen the Cheyenne cowboy back there. They might not recognize him, but I sure do. We locked horns and he scuppered my chance of making big money. I'll never forget that bastard as long as I live.'

Suddenly as the first of the coffins was pushed into the belly of the baggage car the sound of pounding hoofs drew their attention. They all turned and stared at the moonlit rider as Hammer expertly guided the horse beneath him into the stockyard.

Jim Dante stared open-mouthed at Hammer and pointed a shaking arm at the horseman. He did not believe what he was looking at.

'That's the same varmint that you just run over, Bart,' Dante said as he watched the cowboy and clutched Gibbs' arm. 'Who the hell is he?'

Holt spat his cigar at the ground and drew both his guns in one swift action. He cocked their hammers and stepped forward.

'That's the Cheyenne cowboy,' he sneered as he levelled his weapons and aimed at the fearless rider. 'Take a good look at the critter, boys. He'll be dead as soon as my lead reaches him.'

The men huddled around the buckboard watched as Holt squeezed his triggers. Two massive bolts of fiery flame erupted from both his gun barrels and for a brief moment lit up the shadows.

As the ear-splitting noise of the shots echoed around the vast stockyards, a pitiful sound also rang out.

It was the sound of death.

FINALE

Hammer crashed headlong into the wooden fence poles of the cattle pens. He had seen the bright flashes of the guns being fired but it had been too late for him to do anything about it. As his body hit the fence poles he realized what the sickening sound had been and why he had been thrown over the head of the horse. His eyes focused on the horse that had carried him here and saw the mare staggering backwards. The light of the bright moon sparkled on the two bleeding holes in the animal's chest.

The young cowboy got on to his knees and watched as the mare finally succumbed to its fatal wounds. The horse fell lifelessly on to the ground.

More shots exploded behind Hammer. Smouldering sawdust showered over the cowboy as

152

the bullets caught the array of poles between himself and the lethal bunch of wanted men.

Hammer spat at the sand and then moved behind the pens.

Suddenly he was forced to stop. Bullets hit the wooden uprights ahead of him. Hammer sensed that every shot was getting closer and closer to him. He fell on to his face as even more bullets carved through the shadows. He could feel their heat through the back of his shirt. They had him trapped and Hammer knew it.

He reached down and drew his .45.

Looking beneath the poles he saw a trough in the pen. He rolled sideways and then started to crawl forward. Hammer could feel the flesh of both his knees and elbows being grazed as he crawled as fast as he could toward the trough.

Just as he reached the trough Hammer heard galloping hoofs echo behind him as the marshal and deputy led his trail pals into the yard.

Suddenly a volley of nerve-jangling bullets passed over the cattle pens at the five riders.

The Cheyenne cowboy watched helplessly as all five horses reared up. Tapers of impending death splintered through the darkness in search of fresh blood.

Hammer watched as both horses and riders

crashed to the ground in equal portion. It was impossible to tell how many of the riders had fallen victim to the gunmen's lead.

Gunsmoke drifted like a choking fog across the countless cattle pens and Hammer realized that it was time for him to move.

As quickly as he could he hobbled from one pen to another, throwing himself through the gaps between the poles. Hammer knew that the acrid gunsmoke was giving him cover. The cowboy doggedly kept advancing toward the gunmen as they continued to unleash their weapons' venom at the marshal and his men.

The thought of his life savings being stolen somehow kept Hammer moving. The thought of poverty was a far greater spur than the fear of death. Another volley of shots rang out from the men hidden behind the buckboard. They flashed through the shadows like a swarm of crazed fireflies. Hammer dropped on to one knee and watched rested fence poles being reduced to matchwood as bullets impacted into them.

Desperately, the crouching cowboy wondered what he had to do to get the better of the gunmen. Before he had time to come up with a plan, the chilling voice of Holt bellowed across the stockyard.

'I know it's you, Cheyenne,' Holt screamed from

beyond the gunsmoke. 'I recognize your pretty face. Remember me? I'm Emmett Holt. You've got a real bad habit of poking your damn nose into my business. You was lucky last time but not this time. This time I'm gonna kill you.'

Hammer did not reply. He knew Holt was attempting to locate him in the swirling smoke that their guns had discharged. That meant they were not sure where he was and that suited the cowboy just fine.

Shots came from the place he had seen the lawmen and cowboys fall. At least some of them had not been slaughtered, Hammer thought.

'Keep shooting, boys,' he whispered as he turned and focused on the dust coat-clad men beside the passenger car. 'Just keep them busy.'

His mind raced. He knew that his only chance was to somehow get around the side of them. Otherwise it was impossible for him to get the better of men using a buckboard as cover.

He rested his back against a corner fence pole. His eyes searched the shadows and then he stared straight ahead. It dawned on Hammer that he had hobbled at least a hundred yards from where he had been thrown by the horse and was now facing one of the cattle cars.

More shots rang out. Holt and his cohorts were firing blindly, he thought. The bullets were peppering the fencing twenty feet behind his crouching form. His eyes glanced through the gunsmoke and fixed upon the passenger car. There were two cattle cars between him and the men in dust coats, he thought.

His fertile mind started to formulate a crude plan. He knew that it might not work but there was no choice if he wanted to retrieve his savings from Holt and his followers.

The planked cattle cars were rocking as the captive steers within them frantically tried to crash out of the walls. Years of working as a cowboy had taught Hammer that there was nothing more dangerous or unpredictable than terrified cattle. Their fright and instinct for survival made them as deadly as anyone with a six-gun.

The nervous steers wailed like the legendary banshee inside the cattle cars as the gun battle continued to blast across the yard in both directions. Suddenly the cowboy had an idea which he believed just might work.

He rose up to his full height beside the fence poles.

Hammer took a deep breath and lowered his head as his eyes fixed upon the closest cattle car. Steers were ornery animals but the Cheyenne cowboy had a notion that he might just be able to use that temperament against the lethal gunmen.

156

Under the cover of the choking smoke that drifted on the night air, Hammer charged at the cattle car. His momentum was enough for him to launch himself at the high-sided carriage. He flew at the wooden slats and hit the side of the car. His fingers gripped the planks as his boots fought for grip.

He hung there for what seemed like an eternity, then climbed up its planking to where the metal pins secured the large door. Irate steers grunted as he reached the pins. Hammer feverishly pulled one pin from the metal loop that held it in place and then made his way across the side wall to the other metal pin.

Hammer glanced across at the gunmen who were still exchanging shots with Grey and his cronies. A sense of relief washed over the cowboy as it became obvious that they had not seen him.

Using every scrap of his strength Hammer pulled the second pin clear. The massive wooden doorway creaked as it defied gravity and balanced against the bulkhead. Hammer gripped the top of the massive door and pulled it away from the body of the carriage. Like the drawbridge of an ancient medieval castle, the huge door fell heavily toward the ground. The ramp that had been used to load the cattle was now an invitation for the frantic steers to disembark.

Sensing freedom, the steers immediately started to

flee their confines and came down the ramp rapidly. The large beasts scattered in every direction. Several of the mighty animals chose to run along the side of the train toward the buckboard.

Fearing that the gunmen would spot him when they became aware of the freed white-faced steers, Hammer climbed on to the roof of the car and steadied himself. His fears had been correct for no sooner had he reached the roof of the cattle car than a shot tore through the shadows and ripped through the shoulder of his shirt. The cowboy had never felt such pain before. It was like being hit by a red-hot branding iron.

Hammer fell to his knees as blood trickled from the graze. He pulled his gun free of its holster just as Holt blasted another shot up at him.

The bullet flew over his head and the Cheyenne cowboy fanned his gun hammer in reply. He watched as all six of his bullets rained down to where the devilish gunmen were secreted beside the buckboard. To his utter surprise Hammer saw two of Holt's men buckle and fall into the shadowy sand.

Then as he moved away from the edge of the carriage roof to reload his smoking .45 he heard the remaining men scream as a dozen or more of the snorting steers charged into them. The sound of stampeding steers was etched into his memory, just as the screams of men mowed down by raging beasts was also something the cowboy had heard before.

Hammer filled his smoking chambers with fresh bullets from his belt and snapped the rotating cylinder back into the body of his six-shooter. He gripped the gun, crawled to the rim of the cattle car and stared down into the dusty void.

The sickening sight was something he had seen many times before when a herd stampeded and trampled unwary cowboys underfoot. He rose on to his knees and looked down upon the carnage. The steers had trampled the hired gunmen beneath their merciless hoofs. The lamplight from the passenger car highlighted what was left of them. Broken bodies basked in a crimson hue beside the buckboard. Hammer looked up and saw the hoof dust of the running steers as they fled into the depths of the shadowy stockyard.

There was no sense of satisfaction in the cowboy. Just horror and revulsion.

No sooner had Hammer gotten to his feet when he heard something to his left. It was the cocking of a gun hammer. The startled cowboy swung and stared at Holt as the bruised and bloodied gunman clambered on to the roof of the cattle car. With the gun in his hand, Holt straightened up and stood bleeding less than fifteen feet from Hammer.

'Now it's your time to die, Cheyenne,' Holt said as he raised his gun swiftly. Hammer followed suit. Two mighty blasts lit up the night air as both men fired at exactly the same moment.

The gun fell from Holt's grip. He swayed and stared at the young cowboy in disbelief. His eyes looked at the bullet hole in his chest as blood quickly spread across his shirt front.

'You killed me, Cheyenne,' Holt mumbled before staggering backwards and falling between the two cars.

Gat Hammer limped to the edge of the car and looked down at the stricken gunman. Holt's body lay motionless where it had brutally landed. Then Hammer heard his name being called from the approaching lawmen and his fellow cowboys.

He looked down at them and holstered his gun.

He touched his temple in salute.

'It's about time you boys showed up,' Hammer sighed and sat down. His legs dangled over the edge of the carriage as he exhaled. 'I was plumb running out of ideas.'